Third Time's A Charm

ROSE PRESSEY

PRAISE FOR ME AND MY GHOULFRIENDS BY ROSE PRESSEY

ROSE PRESSEY'S COMPLETE BOOKSHELF

Maggie, P.I. Mystery Series:
Book 1 – Crime Wave
Book – Murder is a Beach

The Halloween LaVeau Series:
Book 1 – Forever Charmed
Book 2 – Charmed Again
Book 3 – Third Time's a Charm

The Rylie Cruz Series:
Book 1 – How to Date a Werewolf
Book 2 – How to Date a Vampire
Book 3 – How to Date a Demon

The Larue Donovan Series:
Book 1 – Me and My Ghoulfriends
Book 2 – Ghouls Night Out
Book 3 – The Ghoul Next Door

The Mystic Café Series:
Book 1 – No Shoes, No Shirt, No Spells
Book 2 – Pies and Potions

The Veronica Mason Series:
Book 1 – Rock 'n' Roll is Undead

A Trash to Treasure Crafting Mystery:
Book 1 – Murder at Honeysuckle Hotel

The Haunted Renovation Mystery Series:
Book 1 – Flip that Haunted House
Book 2 – The Haunted Fixer Upper

DEDICATION

This is to you and you know who you are.

ACKNOWLEDGMENTS

To my son, who brings me joy every single day. To my mother, who introduced me to the love of books. To my husband, who encourages me and always has faith in me. A huge thank you to my editor, Eleanor Boyall. And to the readers who make writing fun.

CHAPTER ONE

Being the leader of the Underworld had many challenges. I'd only just started to come to terms with my new status as the witch in charge when Giovanni St. Clair had showed up in the middle of the night and claimed that he was next in line for the position. He was a witch too, and according to him, I was holding the title illegally.

Pinpricks of stars covered the night sky and the darkness added to the spookiness of the situation as we stood in front of the New Orleans Coven's plantation. I felt trapped by the surrounding moss-covered oak trees and bayou just beyond the plantation's boundaries.

Of course with Giovanni's ridiculous statement, I'd told him to get lost. Without proof, I wasn't going to deal with him tonight.

"I'll come for the Book of Mystics soon." He forced an insincere smile to his lips.

I'd always been terrible at guessing people's age, but I figured Giovanni was around thirty-five. He looked dapper in a black suit, a white shirt and a black tie. With one final glare in my direction, he climbed back into his black car and drove off into the night just as mysteriously as he'd come.

Earlier in the evening I'd battled a demon and now I had to deal with a man who wanted my job. Just when I'd thought my night was taking a turn for the better... he'd shown up.

Have you ever felt as if your life was spiraling out of control? Have you ever felt you were falling and there was no way to stop the fall and devastation that was about to happen? Yeah, that was the way I'd felt for the past couple of weeks. My best friend Annabelle Preston said I had a knack for the dramatic, but I seriously didn't think this was an overreaction. I mean, I'd only recently been named leader of the Underworld and in that short time I had already fended off several people who also wanted the title.

Who knew leading the Underworld was such a sought-after position. It came with a lot of responsibility. That was something that shouldn't be taken lightly. I hadn't even figured out what the leader of the Underworld was supposed to do. But I was determined to find out. I wouldn't let someone just come in and steal this title from me. Not if the position wasn't rightly theirs—but now, with Giovanni's claim, I wasn't quite sure. He'd been vague in his declaration and he hadn't given me the opportunity to ask more questions.

Claiming to be the leader of the Underworld was nothing new, but Giovanni alleged that he had proof. I had yet to see that evidence, but apparently he planned to show up at LaVeau Manor with the proof that he needed.

I'd been in New Orleans with Nicolas, Liam, and my best friend Annabelle and her boyfriend-slash-bodyguard. She'd needed a bodyguard ever since one of the aforementioned demons had attacked and threatened her. I'd just fought off a demon with the help of the others. After the fight, I'd appointed Liam the New Orleans coven leader. He'd stayed behind at the New Orleans plantation, which was now his new home because of his coven leader status. I had to admit that I had mixed emotions about his staying behind, but Nicolas was a sweet man and when I was with him I felt swept away with excitement.

Shock fused with anger caused knots to form in my stomach. This whole leader of the Underworld thing had been a headache, but I still wasn't ready to relinquish the title. Of course I would if it rightly belonged to someone else, but I wouldn't unless I absolutely had to. There was no way I'd take a stranger's word for it.

My name is Halloween LaVeau. I was once known around Enchantment Pointe as Worst Witch of the Year. But that had changed when I'd inherited my great-aunt Maddy LaVeau's manor. I shared the place with her black cat Pluto. He wasn't that impressed with my presence, although he was learning to tolerate me more with each fish snack I gave him. It was a creepy place and I hadn't known what to do with the massive structure at first. Then one day it hit me: turn it into a bed-and-breakfast.

On the first night of my new business venture, a mysterious and gorgeous man had shown up at my front door. It had been a dark and stormy evening, like a scene right out of some cheesy Halloween movie.

Then the next day, another gorgeous man had shown up at my front door and I'd known that it hadn't been a coincidence. After all, I wasn't at the top of the Best Bed-and-Breakfasts Ever list, so I knew the strangers were up to something right away. Little had I known that night that the men were actually brothers, and that they were witches and vampires.

Now we were in the car headed back to LaVeau Manor. We'd been at a beautiful plantation which was the home of the New Orleans Coven. I'd had to dismiss the former leader for being involved with black magic and demons. The clouds slowly covered the moon as I stared out the window and up at the sky. Annabelle and Jon Santos sat in the backseat of the car. Jon was another detective with the Underworld. When I glanced back at them, they had shut their eyes and were holding hands.

They made a good couple, but it was still early in their relationship. Not to mention, Annabelle wasn't paranormal and normally wanted no part of it.

Nicolas was behind the wheel. He and his gorgeous half-brother Liam looked alike with thick dark hair, deep blue eyes, high cheekbones and dazzling smiles. They had more than their share of masculinity and irresistible levels of charm.

He smiled at me when I looked over at him. "How are you holding up? You must be exhausted."

"Me? I'm fine. You're the one who should be exhausted. Being held by a demon can be a little draining, right?"

I wished that we could forget what we'd seen and what had happened. All I wanted was a normal evening with Nicolas.

My relationship with Nicolas had gotten off to a strange start. I'd had a tough time working out my feelings for the brothers, Nicolas Marcos and Liam Rankin. It was for the best that Liam stayed in New Orleans. He would be an hour away and that would put the needed distance between us. I wanted to see where things went with Nicolas.

Before the men had arrived, I'd found this old book in the attic. As it turned out, the book allowed the person who owned it to become the leader of the Underworld. Yes, you guessed it… I was the lucky owner. A lot of people wanted to get their hands on this book.

I'd fought off demons and witches for this book. Nicolas and Liam had wanted to get rid of the thing. In hindsight, maybe that wouldn't have been such a bad idea. Not only did the Book of Mystics make me the leader, it also gave me the power to reanimate the dead. Let's just say that hadn't gone well so far. Since I hadn't asked for the job, I wasn't exactly excited about my new talent.

It had brought the aforementioned demon into my life. My substandard spell-casting had accidentally brought back a beautiful blonde disguised as a demon named Isabeau Scarrett. I'd never intended on allowing demons to return to this world; bringing the dead back to life was something I didn't want to do. That was where my questionable spell-casting came into the picture.

Things had been beyond stressful. On top of the demons showing up, I had feelings for Nicolas and, as much as I tried to deny it, there were sparks with Liam too. I'd fought off demons with the brothers during the annual Halloween bash and with all the time that we'd spent together lately, we were quickly growing close as friends.

Then there was the demon witches Jacobson and Sabrina. It was like an endless stream of people wanting to get their hands on the book. Jacobson had been the leader of the New Orleans Coven before I'd made Liam the new leader. Jacobson's sister Sabrina had accused Nicolas of turning her into a vampire, but in reality, the brother and sister had just been trying to get revenge for the vampire that Nicolas and his mother had killed; that vampire had turned Nicolas and his mother many years ago. It wasn't like Nicolas had any other choice. He'd only staked the vampire to save his life.

On top of all that, now I had another witch claiming he had proof that he was the true owner of the book. Soon enough I'd find out if he was telling the truth. I didn't know how, but I wouldn't stop until I got to the bottom of his claim.

The road stretched out endlessly in front of us. The darkness consumed us and the clouds now concealed the moon which had been our only source of light on that lonely stretch of highway leading back to Enchantment Pointe. Our surroundings were eerily peaceful until in a matter of seconds, bright lights appeared directly behind us. I looked over my shoulder and was blinded by what I assumed were another car's high beams.

Nicolas glanced in the rearview mirror. The car continued to follow closely. "I think I'll slow down so this car can pass."

I nodded. "They must be in a hurry," I said.

When Nicolas slowed down, the car didn't pass. It remained behind us, practically touching our bumper.

"Why aren't they passing?" I asked.

Nicolas peered into the rearview mirror again. "I don't know, but there's nowhere for me to pull over and let them pass."

With this driver's obvious road rage, I wasn't sure pulling over would have been a great idea anyway. My anxiety grew and I wondered why this person was driving so erratically. Had they been drinking?

"Maybe we should call the police and report them?" I asked.

Reporting this driver would be for the best. I didn't want to give this person the opportunity to hurt or kill someone. I pulled my phone out and before I had a chance to dial the numbers, the engine roared loudly and the car zipped past. It was dark, but I was sure that the car was black. And I was also sure that I'd seen the vehicle very recently. It looked like Giovanni St. Clair's car. I wasn't surprised that he'd followed us.

CHAPTER TWO

The aggressive driving was Giovanni's way of intimidating me. I couldn't let him get to me. But his driving was close to moving past intimidation and into the dangerous and deadly realm.

"Hey, it's that Giovanni guy." Nicolas' eyes remained fixed on the road ahead.

"Yeah, I don't appreciate that he's trying to scare me," I said.

"As soon as I find a spot to safely pull over, I'm going to confront him," Nicolas said.

The car swerved back into the correct lane and was now in front of us. Giovanni tapped the brakes and the bright red lights glowed ominously in the night. Nicolas slammed on his brakes. My seatbelt locked as my body moved forward and then my head smacked back onto the headrest.

"What's going on?" Jon leaned forward from the backseat.

"Giovanni St. Clair has caught up with us again. He's using his car to scare us now." I inhaled a deep breath and braced myself for what might happen next.

"What does he think he'll accomplish by making us wreck?" Annabelle asked.

When I looked back at her, I knew we both had the same thought. If Giovanni killed me, he might think it would be easier for him to get the Book of Mystics. Maybe that was his plan, but he'd never find the Book of Mystics, I reminded myself.

"What are we going to do?" Annabelle asked.

Nicolas slowed the car down.

"We're not going to stop, right?" Annabelle asked anxiously.

"No, I won't stop," Nicolas said. By his clenched jaw and narrowed eyes, I wasn't sure if I believed him.

For the moment everything was calm as we continued down the road. At least Giovanni wasn't slamming on his brakes. I didn't want to get lulled into a false sense of security though. He could make another erratic movement at any moment. I was on edge waiting for his next move. When I thought I couldn't handle the tension any longer, the car accelerated and disappeared into the night.

I released a deep breath. "Do you think he's gone for good?" I hoped that he wouldn't be waiting for us around the next turn.

Nicolas nodded. "I think he was just trying to scare you. He'll probably leave us alone tonight."

Yeah, he'd leave us alone for now, but I knew it wouldn't last long. I'd be on edge waiting for his next move. The tension was heavy in the car, but after a few minutes with no car in sight, we began to calm down. I leaned my head back on the seat and tried to relax for the rest of the trip.

A million thoughts raced through my mind. It was strange to think about how much things had changed in such a short time. I had a hard time wrapping my mind around how this had happened to me. Why had I found the book? Why not someone else? All my life I'd wanted for my magic to be better, and now I wasn't sure what I wanted any more.

I knew my mother was happy with my improved status in the witchcraft world. Much to my mother's chagrin, I'd never been good at witchcraft. She'd named me Halloween in the hopes that I'd have special magical skills. Unfortunately for her, that had never happened. The only thing that had improved my witchy skills was becoming the owner of the Book of Mystics. Some people claimed that I had to have special magical skills to get the book to work for me, but if *I* had special talents, then I'd hate to see how poorly someone *else* used the book.

No matter what they said, I'd messed up plenty since I'd found the book. The local Coven had always tried to distance themselves from me, but now that I owned the book, they wanted to be a part of my life. I never wanted to be a person to hold a grudge, so I was trying to forgive and forget. I believed that people could change and as long as their hearts were in the right places, then I was willing to forgive. I hadn't blamed them for not wanting me around in the past. My magic had been so bad that I'd made other witches' magic spells go horribly wrong when I performed mine. Witches from miles around would call and complain that my magic casting had interfered with theirs in a negative way.

We finally pulled up to LaVeau Manor. The massive structure had an unquestionable authority as it towered over us. Old oak trees surrounded the manor with branches swaying in the wind. A long pebble driveway stretched out in front of the manor and an old iron gate with stone columns guarded the entrance. My new place was in the town of Enchantment Pointe. It was a small town, but needless to say it had its share of magic. LaVeau Manor sat next to the river and even had a small family cemetery in the back next to the tall moss-covered trees. Annabelle was so creeped out by the place's appearance that I could barely get her to enter, although she'd become braver over the past few days. She'd even made it upstairs for the first time since I'd inherited the place. I think it had something to do with the good-looking Underworld detective whom Liam had assigned to watch out for her. Since someone had wanted me eliminated, I knew they wouldn't think twice about going after my non-magical friend.

"It's been a long night. I'll drive Annabelle home," Jon said.

I nodded. "Thank you all for everything. Annabelle, I couldn't have made it through this without you."

Annabelle hugged me. "That's what best friends are for."

"Call you tomorrow. Love you," I said with a wave.

When my phone rang, Annabelle and Jon paused. I think we all knew that it couldn't be good that my phone was ringing at this time of night. They watched as I pulled the phone out and held it to my ear.

I didn't think to look at the caller ID before answering. If I had, I would have turned the phone off and gone to bed. But I guessed ignoring the problem wouldn't make it go away. Just hearing Giovanni's voice made my stomach turn.

"Good evening, Ms. LaVeau." I imagined that a creepy smile slid across his face.

"It was a good evening until you showed up," I said through gritted teeth.

He chuckled, then said, "If you think you've offended me with your comment, then you're wrong."

"What do you want?" I asked, letting him know that I didn't want to play his game.

"I'm coming to pick up the book," he said matter-of-factly.

I scoffed. "I don't think so. What gives you the right to take my book?"

Nicolas stood beside me, touching my arm. "Is everything okay?" he whispered.

I nodded. Everything would be fine as soon as I got rid of this nutcase on the phone.

"This is something that we can discuss when I get there," he said.

"I told you there is nothing to discuss. I won't keep having this conversation with you," I said through gritted teeth.

"I'll see you soon," he said as if he hadn't heard a word that I'd said.

It was obviously no use talking to him and telling him not to come.

"By the way, I don't appreciate what you did," I said.

"What do you mean? When I showed up at the plantation?" he asked innocently.

"Well, yes, I didn't appreciate that, but that's not what I was talking about. I didn't appreciate you driving like a madman and slamming on your brakes in front of us," I said.

"I have no idea what you are talking about," he said. I heard the snarky tone in his words.

"You don't know anything, do you?" I asked.

"I know that the book is mine," he said.

"What's wrong?" Nicolas asked.

"Giovanni St. Clair is on his way to LaVeau Manor," I said.

CHAPTER THREE

Nicolas and I were sitting in my parlor. I'd tried to make this room more casual and not as museum-like as the rest of the manor. There was an oversized white sofa on one side of the room with chairs placed in front to make a conversational area. It was supposed to be a relaxing room, but that was a tough task to accomplish at LaVeau Manor. No matter the creepiness, I'd started to become more comfortable with the manor. It was my home now.

Silence filled the air. We were too nervous to talk. I just wanted to find out what this man had to say and get on with it. Annabelle and Jon stepped into the room. They'd been out on the front veranda. After I'd received the call from Giovanni, neither Annabelle nor Jon had wanted to leave. I was thankful to have them there for support.

Annabelle touched my arm. "Are you doing okay?"

I nodded. "Yeah, I'll be okay. It's the not knowing that's the hard part. I just want to get it over with."

"This man is probably full of hot air," Jon said.

"Don't worry about it, Hallie. Everything will work out," Nicolas said, squeezing my hand.

A strange feeling gathered in the air. It was like trying to breathe through soup. The others sensed it too because we all exchanged a look. "What's happening?" Annabelle asked.

"It feels like magic," I said.

Nicolas jumped up and rushed over to the window. He peered out across the front lawn and driveway.

"Do you see anything?" I asked, joining him beside the window.

He shook his head. "I don't see anyone, but that doesn't mean they're not out there."

Just when I thought I couldn't be filled with any more dread, this happened. Was someone placing a spell on LaVeau Manor again? We'd just dealt with that when we'd been locked out of LaVeau Manor by Jacobson and his sister, and I didn't want to deal with it again.

"I'm going outside to check it out," Nicolas said.

"I'll go with you," Jon said, following Nicolas out of the room.

Annabelle and I watched from the front veranda as Nicolas and Jon stepped out onto the lawn and then disappeared around the side of the manor.

"I doubt they'll find anything. If someone wants to place a spell on me, they certainly won't let themselves be seen doing it." I tried to control my frustration. I wouldn't let bad witches get under my skin.

"Who do you think it is?" Annabelle asked.

"It could be Giovanni. After all, he said he was on his way here," I said, looking back at the door and worrying about the book.

I knew that it was locked away in a secure location, but that still didn't make me one hundred percent confident that Giovanni wouldn't somehow get the book. I was probably being paranoid, but I couldn't help it.

After a couple minutes, Nicolas and Jon returned.

"Did you see anything?" Annabelle asked.

Nicolas shook his head.

"The strange feeling seems to have disappeared," I said.

"We'll just have to keep an eye out for anything else strange," Jon said.

We stepped back inside and returned to the parlor. I sat back on the sofa and leaned my head back onto the cushion.

"How do you think this man found out that you have the book in the first place?" Annabelle asked.

I threw my hands up. "I'm sure everyone knows by now."

"My mother had a lot of this stuff happen when she first got the book," Nicolas said a little too casually.

"And you're just now telling me this?" I asked with an edge of frustration in my voice.

"Would it have changed anything if I'd told you before?" he asked.

I shook my head. "No. I guess not. There's nothing I can do differently."

Nicolas sat beside me and squeezed my hand. He didn't have to say anything. I felt his concern just by the simple touch of his hand. He lifted my hand to his mouth and placed his soft lips against my skin, delivering tiny kisses up the length of my arm.

The doorbell rang, echoing through the parlor. My stomach flipped and I jumped up from the sofa, making my way to the front door. Footsteps sounded behind me and I knew that everyone was following me to the door.

I peeked out. Giovanni St. Clair stood in front of the door with a smirk across his face. Other than his name, I had no idea who this man was or what made him think that he should be the leader of the Underworld, but it looked as if I was about to find out. Maybe he was the reason for the strange vibe that we'd sensed moments ago.

"Is it him?" Annabelle asked, trying to get a peek out the front door.

"Yeah," I whispered, as if he could hear me through the door.

The heavy wooden door creaked ominously as I opened it, giving us a warning signal that this visitor was nothing but danger.

"Hello, Ms. LaVeau," he said with a devilish grin. His tone was full of disdain.

I was in no mood for pleasantries with this man. He wasn't a bed-and-breakfast guest, so my hospitality responsibilities were out the window.

"Mr. St. Clair." I paused as he stared at me.

I supposed he wanted me to invite him in. I sucked in a deep breath and gestured for him to enter the manor. "Please come in."

It was all I could do to be nice to this man. I supposed if he truly did have a right to the title, I should be nice and not hold it against him, but after all that I'd been through it was hard to deal with. Just in case this man was going to be the leader of the Underworld, I figured I would try to be a little nicer.

"Won't you join us in the parlor?" I pointed toward the room to our left.

He smiled and nodded, then walked toward the room with a strut that let me know he fully expected the title to be his.

"Thank you," he said over his shoulder.

I figured he knew by the scowl on my face that I was trying hard to be nice, but really wanted to tell him to get lost. Nicolas, Annabelle, and Jon followed me into the parlor. Giovanni hadn't waited for me to tell him to have a seat. He'd already taken position at the end of the sofa. I was trying to be civil, but if he thought I was going to serve him tea and cookies, then he was dead wrong.

"So do you want to tell me what you were talking about?" I asked, getting right to the point. The faster we got this over with the faster he would be out of LaVeau Manor and my life.

A wide grin spread across his face. "You get right to the matter, don't you? I like that." He stared me up and down.

Nicolas moved closer, protectively. I felt his body tense.

"I'm sure you can understand that I am suspicious of your claims. I've had to deal with quite a few people who wanted the book since I became the owner," I said.

He nodded. "Oh, I completely understand. But I'm sure you'll understand my position when I tell you that you are in possession of the book illegally."

I didn't like his tone and I didn't like his words either.

"All right. That's enough of your games." Nicolas moved forward and I grabbed his muscular arm. The last thing I needed was for the two of them to fight, although it would be two against one because Jon and Nicolas had been friends for quite some time and I knew he wouldn't let Nicolas take on Giovanni alone.

"What do you mean I am in possession of the book illegally? It was here in my great-aunt's home. She left the place to me, so anything in the home is now mine." I smiled, proud that I could offer him this detail.

"You see, the book was stolen from my mother by a woman named Gina Rochester. I believe you know her," Giovanni said with a smirk.

I stopped in my tracks. That was Nicolas' mother. I glanced at Nicolas and saw the fury in his eyes.

"Are you referring to my mother?" Nicolas asked through gritted teeth. "My mother never took anything in her life. I don't appreciate you suggesting such."

Giovanni leaned back on the sofa and crossed his arms in front of his chest. "Look, I didn't mean to offend, but I'm just telling you the facts."

"I don't believe you and if that's all you've got in the way of proof, then I'm going to have to ask you to leave," I said, crossing my arms in front of my chest.

"Yes, how dare you come in here and accuse someone of stealing. Who do you think you are?" Annabelle said.

She'd really gotten braver and more vocal in the past few days. I was glad to see her coming out of her shell. I needed to follow her lead.

"I didn't come here with merely hearsay," Giovanni said. "I told you I have proof and that's what I have got."

His statement had me more fearful than ever.

CHAPTER FOUR

"How about you explain what you're talking about?" I asked crossly. "You can't come in here and accuse someone of a crime without telling us what brought you to that conclusion in the first place. You especially can't accuse someone who is no longer around to defend herself."

If only Nicolas' mother was still around. She'd been killed by her evil sister. Her sister had of course wanted the Book of Mystics. Nicolas' mother had come back in spirit form to talk with me, but that had taken a great deal of energy and I doubted she'd be able to do it again. I was almost afraid to attempt bringing anyone back with a spell after all the times I'd messed it up. I was going to leave that one alone.

"My mother was Anais St. Clair, née Demarco. She was the owner of the book. It disappeared and then Nicolas' mother became the leader. She stole the book from my mother." He folded his hands together and placed them in his lap.

I held my arm out, blocking Nicolas from moving forward and confronting Giovanni. I knew he didn't want to listen to the man talk about his mother like that, but I had to get to the bottom of what was going on.

"Jon, can you and Nicolas wait for me on the veranda? I'd like to speak with Giovanni alone." I looked at Jon.

Nicolas shook his head. "That's not a good idea, Hallie. Someone should be in here with you."

"I'll be fine," I said as I glared at Giovanni.

Nicolas finally released a deep breath and joined Jon on the other side of the room.

"I'll go outside with the guys," Annabelle said.

"You can stay if you'd like, Annabelle," I offered, hoping that she wouldn't leave.

She shook her head and stared at Giovanni. "I need fresh air anyway."

I didn't blame her. I didn't particularly want to be in the room with this man either. Nicolas hesitated and looked at me again. I nodded and smiled, then he finally walked out with Jon and Annabelle.

Now that I was alone with Giovanni, I could get to the bottom of this without worrying about Nicolas pulverizing Giovanni.

"How do you know that Nicolas' mother took the book? And if your mother had the book, then why wasn't she the leader?" I asked, crossing my arms in front of my chest.

He smiled. "My mother didn't own the book long enough to accept the position as leader. She had it for about an hour."

"How can you prove this?" I asked with a smirk.

"I can prove it to you if you let me see the book," he said.

I scoffed. "Oh, no, do you really think I would fall for something like that? Do you really think I am that stupid?"

He smirked. "I don't think you're stupid. Quite the opposite, actually. You are a smart woman and beautiful too, I might add."

There was no way flattery would get him anywhere. "As soon as I bring the book out you will take off with it."

"I would never dream of doing such a thing," he said innocently.

"We're discussing the details of the book only. This is a serious matter and I think you're aware of the gravity of this situation. I am the leader and I intend on keeping it that way. So I suggest you tell me how it is that you think you own the book and make it snappy. You only have a few minutes before I kick you out." I sat up a little straighter.

He stared at me for a moment and I pointed at the grandfather clock.

Finally, he said, "Only the true owner of the Book of Mystics can add a spell to the book. My mother added a spell to the book, and I can add one too. So you see, Nicolas' mother stole the book. She was never the true leader because she was never able to add a spell to the book. Have you added a spell to the book?" he asked with a condescending smirk.

It felt as if someone had knocked the air right out of me. No, I had not added a spell to the book. How the heck would I do something like that? I'd barely gotten the chance to read the book. The Book of Mystics that I'd found in my great-aunt's attic had been written in a strange language. It had only appeared in English at times when I needed it the most. What would I say to this man? He was staring at me, waiting for an answer.

Finally, I settled on, "I can't give you that information. I'm the leader and I don't have to discuss the book with you. It is a private matter. I am entrusted with holding this book and I plan on keeping it that way."

"I'll take that as a no." He smirked. "That's why I wanted to see the book so that I could show you the spell that my mother added to the book, plus add a spell on my own. Once that's done then you can hand over the book and this whole nasty misunderstanding will be over. And since you had nothing to do with the crime, I won't hold you accountable."

Gee, that was awfully nice of him. Considering I really hadn't done anything wrong.

"Plus, I won't do anything to Nicolas for his mother's actions," he said with a smile.

He was proud of his noble acts. This guy had really rubbed me the wrong way this time.

"Do you expect me to just take your word for it? Even if you can add a spell to the book, I'm going to need more proof that this is actually the law of the book. So I'm sure you'll understand that I need more time to research this," I said.

He took a deep breath and released it. "Fine, but don't take too long. I have to return home soon."

"Where is home?" I asked.

"I live in Baton Rouge," he said.

Nicolas, Jon and Annabelle returned to the room. I supposed they were getting antsy and wanted to know what was happening. How would I ever explain this to them?

Giovanni pushed to his feet. "I'll be in touch very soon." He nodded goodbye and walked toward the door. "I'll see myself out, Ms. LaVeau."

With that, he was gone. And none too soon for me either. But I knew he would be back. I had to figure out if what he said was true. How would I do that? There had to be something in the Book of Mystics on this subject. If I wasn't the owner of the book, then how the heck could I read what was on the pages? Supposedly, only the true owner could read it.

Wasn't there somewhere that the basic laws of magical society were codified? The understanding of the laws was somehow dependent on one person being able to occasionally read snippets from an otherwise indecipherable book? Wouldn't it be easier if they had just written this stuff down in plain English? If no one could read the book, how would they know the leader of the Underworld wasn't lying to them? Heck, I could tell everyone whatever I wanted the book to say. Imagine if I pretended to read from the book that the laws of the Underworld stated that all witches must give me double chocolate chip cookies. Or endless amounts of cupcakes?

Nicolas, Jon and Annabelle stared at me. "Well, what did he say?" Annabelle asked.

"He said that the true owner of the Book of Mystics can add spells to the book. He claims that his mother added a spell and that Nicolas' mother did not. He asked me if I'd added a spell to the book," I said.

Annabelle's eyes widened. "Have you?"

I think she knew me well enough to know that I definitely had not. I gave her the look and she nodded with understanding. "I only just figured out what the book says—well, what some of the book says—and it never mentioned anything about adding spells."

"I don't trust him and he gives me the creeps." Annabelle rubbed her arms.

"Do you all know anything about this?" I asked, looking from Nicolas to Jon.

They shook their heads.

"I intend to find out who that guy is," Nicolas said. "He can't come in here and accuse my mother and get away with it. And I won't allow him to take the book from you either."

Annabelle stepped over to the window and looked out. "He's pulling out of the driveway now."

Nicolas walked over and touched my shoulder as he stood behind my chair.

Annabelle looked at us and said, "We should go. It's been a long day and I know we all need rest."

I nodded. "I'll talk to you tomorrow."

Nicolas and I walked them to the front door and said goodbye. After Annabelle and Jon left, it was just Nicolas and me. He stepped closer and took my hand in his. He

22

traced my lips with his finger, then lowered his mouth to mine. After the passionate kiss, he didn't speak, but instead he guided me toward the staircase. My heart beat wildly in my chest. I followed him up the stairs and to my bedroom.

Nicolas' sexual magnetism was something that I couldn't resist tonight. Nicolas led me over to the large mahogany bed in the middle of the room. The restless desire in his eyes had my heart racing. A small lamp on the nightstand cast a soft glow across the cream-colored walls. He pulled back the white down comforter and I joined him on the soft bed.

My pulse skittered as his hands traced my exposed skin. His touch was soft and delicate. My head went back, exposing my throat to him. His fangs grazed the skin of my neck, and then he kissed me on the lips. My senses reeled as I lost myself his arms. Tonight more than ever I needed to allow myself to be swept away from the chaos. Nicolas was just the person to do this.

CHAPTER FIVE

Nicolas' eyes were closed and his chest moved up and down gently as he slept. I had to admit that I hated getting out of the bed and leaving him, but I wanted to check the book for the spell that Giovanni claimed his mother had added. I wanted to be alone while I did it too. If the outcome was bad news and the book really had an added spell, then I wanted to handle it on my own terms. I'd tell everyone about it later.

Since everyone wanted to get their hands on the Book of Mystics, I had a secret hiding place for the book now. It was in a locked box, in a locked trunk, at the foot of my bed. I kept my bedroom door locked at all times too. I wasn't taking any chances.

After slipping out of bed, I eased across the floor, trying to keep the loose boards from squeaking and waking Nicolas. I glanced over at him. He even looked gorgeous while he was sleeping. I imagined that I drooled or something while I was sleeping—not exactly sleeping beauty.

I finally got the trunk unlocked and grabbed the book. When I reached the bedroom door, I looked back at Nicolas. He was still asleep, so I eased out of the room and tiptoed down the stairs. When the house was completely silent, it felt as if it watched my every move. At first this sensation had been unnerving, but the longer I stayed at LaVeau Manor, the more comfort it gave me. The house had a soul and eyes. If only the walls could talk.

When I reached the bottom of the stairs, my cell phone rang in my purse on the parlor table.

"Who could that be?" I whispered to Pluto as he zipped by. I hurried and pulled the phone from my purse. I recognized the number right away.

"I heard what happened," Liam said when I answered the phone.

"Word gets around quickly," I said.

"Jon called me to give me a heads up. Are you doing okay?" he asked with concern in his voice.

"As well as can be expected, I guess." I looked over my shoulder, sure that I'd heard a sound.

"Do you know anything about his claims? Do you know this Giovanni guy? I've certainly never heard of him," Liam said.

"I've never heard of this rule he claims entitles him to the book, and I don't know who he is either," I said.

"I'll see what I can do to help," he said.

"Thanks, Liam. I know I can always count on you."

"I'll look into it first thing in the morning. How's Nicolas handling it?"

I was shocked that Liam had asked about his brother. They had a rocky relationship to say the least, but since I'd met them, they had made small steps toward mending that broken fence. I liked to think I had a little bit to do with that.

Their problems had started long before I knew them though. The tension between the brothers had been evident from the moment they had arrived at LaVeau Manor. The fact that Liam and Nicolas had the same father hadn't stopped the resentment between them.

They'd kept the fact that they were brothers from me for a long time.

Liam was the Underworld detective who had been in charge of protecting Nicolas' mother. She had been murdered by her sister when Liam had been guarding her, and Nicolas had held that against Liam for some time. At least that was what Liam had thought, but Nicolas had explained that he wasn't holding a grudge.

Nicolas and his mother had been turned by a group of vampires. The same vampires had later turned Liam. The two men had taken their time telling me that they were vampires—the truth had only come out when they could no longer hide their fangs.

"Nicolas is doing okay." I'd failed at hiding the surprise in my voice.

"Just let me know if you need anything, okay?" Liam's voice was low and sexy.

He seemed a million miles away now. It had only been a short time ago that he'd been in my bed where Nicolas was now. No, it wasn't how it sounded. He'd only been protecting me and nothing had happened, but I wouldn't lie and say that I hadn't thought about it at the time. We had shared several passionate kisses. How was I supposed to choose between two gorgeous men?

"Thank you," I said softly. "I'll see you soon, okay?"

"I'm looking forward to it," he said, then hung up.

Uh-oh. What was I doing? What had I gotten myself into? This was why my life was spiraling out of control. Leading the Underworld, fighting demons, and having two sexy men in my life—I had to figure things out pronto.

After stuffing the phone back into my purse, I carried the book into the kitchen and placed it on the island in the center of the room. The kitchen was a sea of white. My aunt Maddy's apothecary jars filled with spices and herbs lined the shelves to my left and a stone fireplace with a large cauldron was on the wall to my right. Just down the hallway was the large dining room. A massive mahogany dining table sat in the middle of the room with an equally impressive crystal chandelier dangling above it.

It seemed like forever ago that I'd served Liam and Nicolas breakfast on that first day. If I'd known then what I knew now, would I have run away? Would I have given the Book of Mystics to someone else? Maybe that would have ended all the headaches I was now dealing with. Yet here I was trying to keep the book out of Giovanni's hands. Apparently I enjoyed being the leader more than I realized, or I was just asking for stress.

I flipped open the front cover of the large leather-bound book. As soon as my fingers touched the pages the words turned from a language that I didn't understand to English. Now if I could just find what I was looking for. I needed to check the book for spells that had been added recently. But how would I know? They all looked old and as if they'd been there for ages.

I flicked through the pages, but since I couldn't read everything in the book, I had no idea which spell had been written by whom. Only the spells that the book felt I needed would appear to me in English. Directions and instructions were now in English, but I saw no mention of adding spells. And as far as I knew, there was nowhere in the book that it stated who had written a particular spell. Anyone could claim that they had written the spell, but how would they prove it?

"Why can't you help me now when I need it the most?" I said to the book.

Great, now I was actually talking to the book. Thank goodness it hadn't talked back.

A wind soon whirled around me and the pages of the book flipped rapidly. After a few seconds, the wind stopped and the book had come to rest on a page toward the back.

I had no idea what the spell was for, but apparently the book was trying to guide me in the right direction. Not any easy task, I had to admit. With my way of constantly screwing things up, it would be much easier if the spells were labeled with names. At least then I would have some idea of what I was getting myself into.

I'd gotten used to some of the spells already, and it looked as if this one was for clarity—maybe to help with my thoughts as I figured out this mess. For the spell, I'd call to the elements. Rising my arms and facing north, I recited the words: "Element of Earth, I call to you. Empower me with your energy to see clearly." I moved to face the west, and recited the words: "Element of Air, I call to you to push away the negativity that surrounds me." Once again I changed positions so that I now faced the south and recited the words: "Element of Fire, I call to you for warmth and protection. Help me have the knowledge." With one more move I faced the east and recited the words: "Element of Water, I call to you for force and tranquility. Give me the force to make the right decisions."

Energy pulsated around me for several seconds, then began to fade. When I positioned myself over the book again, another blast of wind whipped through the room.

I recited the words: "Allow this spell to carry away the bad. Allow this spell to banish distraction. This spell will only allow the good in. The spell will carry negativity away. Away with the bad and negative, bring in clarity. Give me the power to fight evil."

It was never clear right away if the spells I'd cast had worked, but it wouldn't take long for me to figure out if I'd performed the spell incorrectly. With my lousy spells, I wouldn't blame anyone for betting against me.

As I closed the book, a sudden sense of someone watching me fell over me. I hadn't heard Nicolas moving around upstairs, so I assumed he was still asleep. With my record, I wouldn't be surprised if I hadn't reanimated someone again. Why did the book keep giving me spells that brought back spirits?

Well, technically I had been responsible because I kept messing up the spells. That was probably the case this time as well. If I couldn't get the spells right, then I needed to stop trying. There came a time when everyone needed to admit they sucked at a certain thing. Like my mother with crafts, bless her heart. She tried to be crafty, but she usually ended up with third-degree burns from the glue gun and a craft item that no one could identify.

I paused, hoping that the sensation would pass, but it wasn't going away. I knew I'd have to turn around and see if there was someone behind me. It wasn't something I was looking forward to though.

I couldn't avoid it any longer though because a woman cleared her throat behind me. I knew it was a woman because it was a soft delicate sound. I sucked in a deep breath and steadied myself for what I was about to see.

When I slowly turned around, it was as if the wind had been knocked out of me. I had been expecting to see a woman standing behind me—a spirit whom I'd reanimated and who now had a second chance on earth. But nothing could have prepared me for what I saw this time.

CHAPTER SIX

It wasn't a woman standing behind me. It was a group of women, all dressed with clothing that appeared to be from sometime in the 1700s. They wore witches' hats—big black witch hats. It was as if I'd stepped into a costume party, only I hadn't invited these guests. They wore long black dresses that buttoned up to their necks. An odd symbol was embroidered on the side of the dress near the waist. It was a knot with smaller knots circling it. They stared at me expectantly, as if waiting for me to explain my actions. They didn't look particularly friendly, but that fact didn't really surprise me.

"Hello," I said calmly. I didn't want to scare them and cause any sudden movements or crazy spells.

"What have you done?" one of them scolded me.

The woman shook their fists at me. Their eyes narrowed as their gazes locked on my face.

"What are you doing here?" I asked.

"Why are you asking us that? You should tell us why you brought us here... and in the middle of the night too. This had better be important," one of the women said, shaking her finger in my direction.

Wow, they'd been here for two seconds and they were already angry with me. The women appeared to be in the age range between thirty and fifty—one of them tall, one of them short and the others in between. A couple had dark hair and the other two had light hair. All of them wore scowls on their faces. They didn't look happy with me for bringing them here.

"I'm sorry about the time. I didn't bring you here on purpose," I said.

The woman standing in the front who I assumed was the leader let out a loud huff. "You mean to tell me you dragged us back here and you don't even need us?"

"Oh, I didn't say that. I mean, I don't know what I need." I was completely rattled now.

"I told you that these modern witches don't know what they're doing. They need to go back to the old-fashioned way of doing things," the shortest woman said.

"It's from buying store-bought spices and herbs. They should grow their own," the other woman said.

I waved my arms to get their attention. "Before you all get mad at me for not growing my own herbs, will you please tell me who you are?"

"My name is Rebecca Greene," the woman said.

Rebecca had a stern face with what looked like a permanent scowl. Her brown hair was twisted into a tight up-do with her hat pointing toward the sky as if it had been starched within an inch of its life.

"This is Kimberly Adams." She gestured toward the tall dark-haired woman to her right.

The woman had thick glasses and offered a half-hearted lopsided grin. "Hello."

"Over there is Barbara Crane," Rebecca said.

The petite blonde woman gave a little wave. Well, at least she was a little friendlier than Rebecca. Maybe they were starting to thaw their icy demeanor.

"And that is Sarah Kirkpatrick." Rebecca pointed to her right.

The brunette with the long curly hair scowled and shook her head in disapproval. Okay, maybe the iciness was still there.

I threw my hands up. "Look, ladies, I didn't bring you here on purpose and I'm sorry if there was some kind of mix-up. I'll figure out which spell will send you back and you all can be on your way."

Rebecca shook her head. "Oh, no. It doesn't work that way. If we are here then it was meant for us to be here. Apparently you need our services."

I stared at her. "What exactly are your services?"

"We are the Enchantment Pointe Coven," Rebecca offered.

My eyes widened. "I know the Enchantment Pointe Coven and you all are *not* members of that coven."

Rebecca placed her hands on her hips. "Well, of course we aren't *now*, but back in 1785 we were most definitely coven members. Unfortunately, we were hanged for practicing witchcraft."

I was back to my life spiraling out of control again. This was crazy. "But why would you be here now? What could you possibly help me with?" I asked.

Barbara looked over my shoulder. I twisted around prepared to see another reanimated spirit, but there was no one behind me. I turned back around. "What?"

She was still staring at me. "You have the Book of Mystics? Are you the leader of the Underworld?" she asked, pointing at the book still on the counter.

The women's eyes widened as they waited for my answer.

"You mean the Underworld was around back then?" I asked.

"Oh, it's been around for a long time. I don't know how long, but it was very much in existence when we were alive," Rebecca said.

I released a deep breath. "To answer your question, yes, I am the leader of the Underworld."

They stared at me incredulously.

Rebecca said, "Well, we're sorry if we've been rude, but you have to understand that it is a strain on us to come all this way."

I nodded. "I'm sorry again, but the book has a mind of its own sometimes."

She scowled. "I never knew another leader to have any problems with the spells."

I frowned. "Yeah, well, I'm still learning my way around the spellcasting thing."

"You don't look that young. You should have figured it out by now," Barbara said.

I wasn't going to have this conversation with them tonight. I was too tired to debate my bad witchcraft skills. What would Nicolas say when he saw these women?

"Well, apparently we are here for a reason. We have to figure out what that is and remedy it so we can leave," Rebecca said.

The women nodded in unison. I bet I wanted them to leave more than they wanted to leave.

Rebecca looked around the room, then said, "But it is late and I am not doing anything tonight. We will rest for the evening and start fresh first thing in the morning."

What was I supposed to do with a group of four women? They'd have to share rooms. The only paying guests I'd ever had in my bed-and-breakfast were Nicolas and Liam. And that had only lasted a short time. I couldn't ask them to pay now. So technically, if I didn't get a paying guest soon, I wouldn't be able to afford to pay the light bill.

I released a deep breath. "Fine. I guess you'll have to stay here for the night."

"Well, you certainly can't expect us to stay outside," Kimberly huffed. The woman cackled and the sound echoed across the room.

"Don't be too loud," I said, holding my index finger up to my mouth.

"Do you have any guests at the moment?" Sarah asked.

The women looked at me expectantly for an answer.

"Yes, I do have a guest, and he is sleeping. I'll show you to your rooms," I said.

I motioned for the women to follow me up the stairs. Their heavy black boots echoed across the floor as they marched behind me.

"I hope you'll be comfortable in the rooms," I said, trying to make small talk. I wasn't sure what to say. There was a bit of time gap. We probably couldn't chitchat about current events.

"I'm sure they'll be adequate," Rebecca said.

I glanced over my shoulder and gave a little smile. She didn't return the sentiment. That scowl was permanently on her face. There was probably nothing I could say that would make her smile. With their cold personalities, I definitely didn't want them to hang around for long, so I'd have to find a way to get rid of them.

Once we reached the second floor, and I motioned for the women to follow me down the hallway, they stopped. I turned around and looked at them.

"Is something wrong?" I asked.

"What is on the third floor?" Rebecca asked, pointing up.

"There are a couple rooms up there, but that is where my other guest is staying."

I didn't want to tell them that my other guest was really staying in my room. There was no reason they needed to know that. Now if I could just keep them from waking Nicolas.

"Why aren't we staying up there?" Kimberly asked.

"Because you're staying down here," I said matter-of-factly.

With that, I continued my way down the hall, not giving them a chance to ask more questions about the third floor. Why were they interested in the third floor, anyway? Had they sensed something? Did they know about the history of the LaVeau Manor attic? I needed them on the same floor as me so that I could keep an eye on them. I'd learned that from previous experience. Not to mention that the access to the attic was on the third floor. After finding the book up there, I wasn't sure what else would be in that room, so it was off limits to everyone unless I went with them. I didn't trust these women already and they'd only been here ten minutes.

When we reached the first door on the left, I stopped and opened the door. I stepped into the room and the women followed along behind me. A large wooden-framed bed covered with a rich burgundy comforter and plush pillows sat against the middle of the far wall. A small table and burgundy velvet-covered chair was by the window.

"Rebecca, you can stay here with Kimberly if you'd like. I can put Sarah and Barbara in the room down the hall," I gestured toward the hall.

"Sarah snores," Barbara said. "I don't want to stay in the same room with her."

"I do not snore. You take that back," Sarah said.

Barbara shook her fist. "I will not take that back. How do you know you don't snore? You're sleeping and you can't hear yourself."

Their bickering was surely going to wake Nicolas.

Rebecca released a heavy sigh. "Sarah can stay with me. I can sleep through any noise."

"There are towels in the bathroom." I stepped over and opened the door. "The sheets are clean on the bed," I offered.

She nodded, then said, "That will be adequate."

I shrugged and stepped over to the door. "Follow me, Barbara and Kimberly."

I motioned over my shoulder and the women trailed along behind me as I made my way down the hallway. When I reached the bedroom at the end of the hall, I opened the door and motioned for the women to enter.

I wasn't being the best hostess, but it was hard when you'd accidentally conjured up guests. The women stepped into the room hesitantly. It was basically like the other room, other than the comforter was rose-colored, so there wasn't much to explain.

"The linen closet has towels too." I pointed at the bathroom.

Kimberly ran over and snatched the piece of chocolate off the pillow that I'd left. She un-wrapped the gold package then popped the candy into her mouth. She groaned in delight as she chewed. With a mouth full of chocolate, she asked, "What will we have for breakfast?"

I hadn't thought about what I would prepare in the morning. I wasn't even sure I had enough groceries left to feed that many people. "We'll have pancakes and bacon," I said.

Kimberly's eyes widened. "I love bacon." She hurried over and snatched the other piece of candy from the pillow before Barbara had a chance to pick it up. She popped it in her mouth before Barbara could snatch it away. She smacked her mouth as she chewed the candy.

When she finally swallowed, she looked at me and asked, "Do you have snacks?"

I stared for a moment, then said, "Well, you're welcome to anything in the kitchen."

I was hesitant about having the women in the kitchen without me, but I couldn't stay away from Nicolas much longer—he'd come looking for me soon. I knew he would see the women in the morning, so I wasn't sure why I thought I could hide them from him. I might as well go ahead and tell him before he saw the coven members. He knew my magic wasn't perfect, but apparently he liked me in spite of that—at least I hoped he did.

"Please don't do any magic in the kitchen," I said, giving them a stern look.

Their mouths dropped in unison. Barbara said, "I can't believe that you would imply that we will be rude houseguests."

The women stared at me. No matter if they were offended; I wasn't taking any chances this time.

"I didn't say that, but I don't want you doing any magic. Okay?" I said with a wave of my finger.

Finally, they nodded, but the mischievous smiles on their faces made me wary.

After a second, I turned and walked out of the room. I hoped they followed my instructions. Walking past the other bedroom, I contemplated issuing the same warning to Rebecca and Sarah, but the room was quiet, so I figured they'd already turned in for the night. I'd just have to trust that they would behave.

As I stepped into my bedroom, Nicolas turned in the bed and looked at me. I'd wondered how he'd slept through all the action.

He looked at me with groggy eyes. "What's going on? Is everything okay?"

His bare chest was exposed and the sheet covered the rest of his well-muscled body. Okay, he looked sexy everywhere, but especially in my bed. The glow from the small light in the bathroom glimmered over his handsome face.

I shook my head and he sat up as if he'd been poked with a hot poker.

"What's going on?" he asked.

I sat on the edge of the bed next to him. "It's okay. It's just that we have a few guests."

"Oh, you have customers?" he asked.

I released a deep breath and said, "Not exactly."

He frowned. "Tell me everything."

I climbed into bed and curled up next to him and began recounting the story.

"So once again I didn't use my best judgment and performed a spell. In my defense, I really felt like the book was trying to help me. I'm beginning to wonder whose side this book is truly on. But anyway, when I cast the spell…" I sucked in a deep breath, then released it slowly. "I reanimated an entire coven."

His eyes widened. "An entire coven? Where are they now? Did you send them back?"

I shook my head. "No, they don't want to go back. Figures, right? They said that obviously they are here to help me for a reason and until they figure out what that reason is, they aren't going anywhere."

"Maybe they are here to help you figure out whether spells have been added to the book like Giovanni claimed," he said as he caressed my arm.

I shrugged. "Could be. I just hope I figure it out soon. Giovanni will be back and I won't have an answer. I'll have no choice but to give him the book, right?"

Nicolas wrapped his arms around me. "Under no circumstance will you give him that book. I'll take care of him, okay?"

"I don't want you to fight with him," I said.

"I won't fight. I'll handle it in a civilized manner. I promise," he said with a grin. Nicolas touched my cheek with his fingers. "What are the women doing now?"

"I gave them rooms for the night. They wanted to rest and said we can figure out the problem in the morning after we have a fresh start," I said.

"That sounds like a good idea to me." He pulled me and I landed on top of him. My body tingled when my skin touched his. Nicolas rolled me over and embraced me in a kiss.

CHAPTER SEVEN

The sunlight streaming across my face woke me the next morning. It only took a few seconds for the memories of the night before to come floating back to me. Had I been dreaming? It had to have been a dream. I looked over and discovered that Nicolas was not in the bed with me. I had no idea where he'd gone this early, but I hoped he hadn't run in to the coven members on his way out.

After slipping into my clothing, I eased out into the hallway. Both bedroom doors were open and the bed was made in the room across from me. It was the room where I'd placed Rebecca and Sarah. Now I really was questioning my sanity. It had all seemed so real. There was no way I could have dreamed that vividly, right? I was questioning everything that I thought was real.

Moving over to the bedroom down the hall, I peered in and saw that the bed was made in that room as well. Just as I was turning around, something caught my eye. It was a gold wrapper on the floor beside the bed. I recognized it right away. The gold paper was from the chocolate candy that I'd left on the pillows. Now I remembered leaving the candy there and Kimberly eating them as if she hadn't eaten in ages... well, I guess she hadn't.

Then I hadn't dreamed it after all. Were the women still hanging around though? I needed to find out right away. I checked each room of the house and didn't find any sign of the women. And Nicolas wasn't around either.

Since it appeared that I was all alone in the house, I decided to once again take the Book of Mystics downstairs to see if I could find the spells that Giovanni claimed had been added. With any luck, I wouldn't conjure up any more of the dead.

I made my way across the quiet house, placed food in Pluto's dish, then climbed up onto a stool and set the book on the counter in front of me. Maybe things would make more sense in the light of day. As I opened the cover and studied the pages, the book sprang into action and the pages flipped again. This time the book took me to another spell.

You would think that after bringing an entire coven back to life that I would have thought twice about doing another spell, but you'd be wrong. It was like I never learned my lesson. I guess I just kept holding out hope that things would work out right the next time I cast a spell. Unfortunately, each next time never worked out and the cycle of bad magic continued.

When I finished the spell, nothing happened. Well, nothing magical seemed to happen. However, there were four witches standing in the kitchen, glaring at me. They were still dressed in period clothing. If they were going to be here long then I'd have to find them new clothing so that they didn't draw too much attention. But I hoped that they would be leaving today.

"What are we having for breakfast?" Rebecca asked with her arms crossed in front of her chest.

The women nodded in agreement. Obviously they were hungry and I was expected to provide food immediately. I pulled ingredients for pancakes from the shelf and prayed that I didn't burn them.

It was funny how one minute I'd been living a normal, boring life—casting a little spell here or a little spell there—but now I was making breakfast for a coven of witches from the 1700s.

"Aren't you a little too savvy for witches who have been dead for two hundred and fifty years?" I asked as I flipped a pancake.

At least I'd improved my cooking skills… slightly. I'd only burned half the pancakes. After wiping pancake batter off my hands, I poured myself a glass of orange juice.

"We may be dead, but that didn't mean we couldn't see what was going on around us. We know about iPhones, Honey Boo Boo, and peanut butter Pop-Tarts."

I spit out my orange juice; I hadn't expected her answer.

"Are you okay?" Sarah patted me on the back.

I coughed a few times, then managed to say, "I'm fine now."

I gathered the breakfast items, placed them on a tray and carried them into the dining room. When I turned around, the women were standing directly behind me again. Louder footsteps sounded from behind us and I whirled around. Nicolas' smiling face was looking back at me. He wore faded jeans that were low on his hips and a button-down navy shirt. He looked around at the woman. They straightened as they looked him up and down.

Silence as thick as mud hung in the air. Why were the women looking at him like they'd never seen a man before? Their eyes widened as they stared at him.

Finally, when I was just about to speak, Rebecca stepped forward. "Who might this be?" she asked.

"Ladies, this is…" I paused, trying to think of my next words.

Who was Nicolas to me? My boyfriend? I hadn't introduced him since we'd taken our relationship to the next level. We also hadn't had the important conversation as to what we called each other. Was he just a friend?

After the long pause, I finally said, "This is my boyfriend, Nicolas Marcos."

Nicolas smiled and a wave of relief fell over me.

"Your boyfriend? You didn't tell us you had a man friend," Rebecca said.

"This is your suitor?" Sarah asked.

I nodded. "Yes, but I didn't think it was something that you all needed to know."

Barbara scoffed. "Well, it would have been nice if you'd shared this information with us."

Rebecca stared at Nicolas again. I knew the scrutiny from the coven was making him uncomfortable. Heck, it was making me feel weird too. I was sorry for putting Nicolas in this situation.

Finally, she tapped her finger against her lip and then walked a circle around him. "He'll do."

What was that supposed to mean? Nicolas gave an uneasy smile.

"He'll do for what?" I asked.

Rebecca waved off my question. She might not have felt it was important to tell me, but I thought it was of great significance. I wouldn't have blamed Nicolas if he had taken off running out of the manor.

The women grabbed his arms and guided him over to the table. "Please sit at the table and enjoy this wonderful breakfast with us," Barbara said.

The women cackled as Nicolas took a seat. Nicolas chuckled, but it wasn't a fun laugh, more of a 'get me out of here' laugh. I didn't know what the witches were up to, but I wouldn't let anything bad happen to Nicolas.

"Look, ladies, I don't know what scheme you all are thinking of, but Nicolas is off limits for any little games. So leave him alone or you will not be happy with the outcome," I said with a stern voice.

They glared at me, but finally backed away from Nicolas.

He gave a half-hearted smile, then said, "Breakfast looks wonderful. How about we enjoy it before it gets cold?"

"That's a good idea. Breakfast is ready for you all." I pointed at the food on the giant mahogany table.

Annabelle would be proud that some of the pancakes had turned out edible.

"Please have a seat, ladies. I have bacon, eggs, and fruit, too. There's maple syrup and blueberry too." I pointed around the table at the items.

"We haven't eaten a breakfast like this in years," Kimberly said as she piled food onto her plate. "I could eat this whole table of food."

That was probably an understatement; by the look in her glazed-over eyes, it looked as if she could eat three tables full of food. The women pulled out chairs and sat around the table. They batted their eyelashes at Nicolas and giggled.

Within seconds, they were grabbing food and piling it on their plates. Rebecca swirled half the bottle of syrup on her pancakes. Barbara shoved three strips of bacon in her mouth at once.

I stared with my mouth open. "I can make more, ladies, if you all need it." Although from the look of the way they were putting away the food, I wasn't sure that I could afford to feed them. Nicolas stared with his mouth open too, but he didn't say anything.

"Obviously, the Book of Mystics thinks you need us, but why do you think you need our help?" Rebecca asked with scrambled eggs stuffed into her mouth. A few crumbs spilled out as she spoke.

I handed her a napkin, then said, "I don't know why you're here, but I can tell you about something that happened right before you all got here."

"Let's hear it," Barbara said, then shoved a forkful of pancakes into her mouth. Syrup dripped down the fork and onto her arm. She licked the syrup off her skin. I stared, unable to take my eyes off the train wreck.

"We're waiting," Rebecca said, while waving a strip of bacon through the air.

I finally snapped out of the trance and said, "A man showed up and said that he was the true owner of the Book of Mystics. He said that only the true owner can add spells to the book and that his mother added a spell." I released a deep breath then continued, "I haven't added a spell—heck, I can barely do the spells, much less add one. Anyway, Nicolas' mother was the leader before me, but she was killed." I gestured toward Nicolas.

The coven members gasped. "How tragic," Sarah said. "We're terribly sorry."

Nicolas nodded and continued to stare in awe of the women's table manners.

"My great-aunt Maddy had hidden the Book of Mystics after the leader's death, and now that I found it, the book is mine. Apparently, I have the skills to unlock the book's magic, but I can't add spells to the book. Have you ever heard of anything like that?" I asked.

They shook their heads in unison.

"No, we've never heard of that, but that doesn't mean that's it's not true," Rebecca said.

"I'm sure things have changed over the years," I said.

"Could I have a look at the book?" Rebecca asked.

I wasn't sure I trusted her. Heck, I felt like I couldn't trust anyone anymore. The way I felt suspicious of everyone was sad, but true. I guess I'd have to take the chance and let her look at the book though. I needed her advice because at this point it was all I could get. I'd just have to be on guard in case she tried anything funny.

I pushed to my feet. "I'll go get the book."

Nicolas looked at me as if he was pleading for me not to leave him alone with these women.

"I'll be right back." I gave a sympathetic smile and rushed out of the room.

Once upstairs, I grabbed the book from my hiding spot. As I came out of the bedroom, the sound of chatter came from down the hall. I paused and listened. It sounded like chanting. As if the witches were reciting a spell. I knew that I'd left them downstairs. When I walked down the hall, I noticed that their room doors were open. The voices had stopped and there was no one in sight. Figuring it must have been my imagination, I headed downstairs with the book under my arm.

CHAPTER EIGHT

When I returned to the dining room, Nicolas looked even more uncomfortable then when I'd left him. The women were in the middle of asking him twenty questions.

"Are you going to marry her?" Rebecca asked.

Nicolas' eyes widened and he looked as if he'd seen a ghost. "I don't…" he stammered.

Oh, for heaven's sakes. It was way too early to ask about marriage. I hardly knew Nicolas, and I wasn't sure about my feelings for him.

"Here's the book," I announced as I entered the room.

A look of relief spread across Nicolas' face. "I think I'll go for a walk," he said, pushing to his feet. "I'll be back soon." He kissed me lightly on the lips, lingering for just a moment.

I felt the women's eyes on me and I turned around to glare at them.

"You all scared him away," I said as he walked out of the room.

They looked at each other. "How could we possibly do that?"

I waved off the question. "Never mind."

"Let's see the book," Rebecca said, pointing toward the table.

I walked over and placed the book onto the table. If they pointed out the spell that had been added, I'd be forever grateful. I flipped open the cover and they gathered around, looking over my shoulder as if they were afraid to get too close.

"Can you flip to the back of the book?" Rebecca asked.

She wiggled her finger and motioned for me to move the pages. I did as she asked and moved to the back of the book.

"Now flip through a few more pages. If the spell was added recently, the witch would have started at the back," Rebecca said.

"Well, I could have guessed that much," I said.

She scowled and asked, "Is that right? Well, did you try checking at the back of the book yet?"

"Well, no, not yet. Besides, how will you know if a spell has been recently added?" I asked.

"I have my ways," Rebecca said matter-of-factly.

"Didn't you say that you can't read all the spells?" Barbara asked.

"Yes, that's what I said. Can you?" I asked.

"No, I can't. Only the leader can," she said.

I shook my head. This conversation was going nowhere.

"There is a symbol that will stand out if you are familiar with the way the spells are written," Rebecca offered. "I'm assuming you're familiar with the language of the spells by now."

She quirked a brow when I frowned.

"Well, that's an important detail you should have shared to begin with," I said.

She scowled. "Don't blame me. You should know these things."

"Okay, you can't read the spell, but are you familiar with the way the spells are listed on the page?"

The other women gathered around us, but continued to eat their breakfast. I'd never seen anyone eat pancakes without a fork before.

I was expecting another dirty look from Rebecca, but instead she stared blankly for a moment, then said, "As a matter of fact, yes, I am familiar with the way the spells are listed."

"How do you know?" I asked.

"I knew the alchemist who helped write the book." Rebecca pointed at me.

"An alchemist? He helped write the book?" I asked.

"Yes, your great-great-great-grandfather, I believe," she said without looking at me.

My eyes widened. "That's another important detail you should have admitted to sooner. You knew him? How did you know him? I thought he disappeared. Do you know what happened to him?"

She looked away. "I do not know what happened to him. I'm sorry."

Obviously there was something she didn't want to discuss. She wasn't being completely honest with me. I'd have to press for more information later. What was the story behind my great-great-great-grandfather and the Book of Mystics?

"Here's the symbol. It's kind of like an initials stamp," she said, pointing at the book.

I flipped through a few more pages, looking for this supposed stamp. Nothing was popping out at me.

"Right there. That one has the stamp." She pointed.

I stopped on the page and peered down at the words. It was written in the strange language that had become so familiar, yet unfamiliar to me. The spell wasn't changing for me this time. If Rebecca claimed this was a new spell, then I had to find out what the spell was for and what the spell did.

Maybe once I discovered that, I could find out if Giovanni's mother had added the spell to the book. Not only that, but I needed to know more about Giovanni and his mother. Who was his mother? Was it true that only the rightful owner of the Book of Mystics could add a spell? I peered down at the spell which Rebecca claimed had recently been added. Giovanni's claim had to be the truth, right? Why else would the spell be there?

My phone rang, breaking me from the contemplation. "Don't touch that book," I warned as I hurried toward my cell. Peering down at the screen, I saw that it was Liam calling. I hoped that he was having an easy time now that he was the leader of the New Orleans Coven.

"I hope you're calling with good news," I said.

There was a pause and Liam let out a deep breath.

"That wasn't the response I'd hoped for."

"Do you want the good news or bad news first?" he asked.

Normally, I would ask for the bad news first and get it over with, but after the recent string of dreadful events, I needed a little good news to soften the blow.

"I'll take the good news first," I said.

"I found out very little about Giovanni." He paused. "But I have a bigger problem."

There was the bad news that I hadn't wanted to hear. He hadn't wasted any time letting me have it. That couldn't bode well for me.

"What is the bigger problem?" I asked in spite of not wanting to hear the news.

"There's a woman here who claims to be a part of a coven." He rushed his words.

For a moment the room spun. Had I heard him correctly?

"What coven is she with?" I asked, fearing the worst. My voice was barely above a whisper.

"Enchantment Pointe, but not from the coven you know," he said in a low voice.

My stomach dropped. "I can explain."

"What? What do you mean?" He continued before waiting for me to answer. "The strange thing is she claims to be from the Eighties."

"They said they are from the 1700s."

"Who are 'they'?"

"The coven members."

"What are you talking about?"

I released a deep sigh, then said, "Last night I accidentally reanimated a coven from the 1700s. I thought that was who you were talking about."

"No, this woman says she died in 1986."

"You're kidding. Why is she there?" I asked.

"I don't know. She just popped up in the living room last night. One minute I was reading a book and the next I was looking at this woman standing in front of me," he said.

"What time did this happen?" I asked.

It couldn't be possible, right? There was no way that I had made another person pop up at his house with that one spell, right?

He paused, then said, "Actually, it was right after I got off the phone with you," he said.

That definitely wasn't the answer I had hoped for. It looked like my bad magic had struck again.

I glanced over my shoulder again to see if anyone had slipped up behind me. Luckily, I was still alone. "What did she say?"

"Well, needless to say, she's a little confused. I told her that I would call you."

Of course the first person he thought of when a random spirit was reanimated was me. Didn't that happen to anyone else? No, of course it didn't happen to anyone else.

"I guess I should meet her," I said around a sigh.

"I can bring her to you," he said hesitantly.

"Yeah, okay. I'll talk to her."

Sure, he just wanted to get rid of her. Now I would have yet another guest.

"I'll see you soon, okay?" he said in his soothing tone.

My heart skipped a beat when he said he would be here soon. An image of Nicolas' face popped into my head. The coven members really knew how to get rid of a guy. What would they do when they saw Liam? It would be twice as much fun for them.

I'd just hung up the phone when a knock sounded on the door. Jumping up, I eased over to see who was there. Relief washed over me when I saw Annabelle standing in front of the door. I'd told her many times just to come on in, but she never wanted to risk being in the manor by herself. I opened the door and motioned for her to hurry in.

"How's everything going?" she asked as she brushed a strand of blonde hair behind her ear.

Annabelle wore the jeans she'd bought online a few weeks ago and a silky beige blouse. Her makeup and hair were perfect as usual. I hadn't had a chance to call her to tell her about my guests. It had been late and when I'd fallen into Nicolas' arms, well, I'd kind of forgotten about everything. Before I had a chance to tell her about my new guests, I knew that the women had walked up behind me because Annabelle's blue eyes widened as she looked over my shoulder.

I gave a half-hearted smile. "They're behind me, aren't they?" I asked.

She sucked in a deep breath and nodded. "There's only one woman behind you. Who are they?" she whispered.

"Hello," Rebecca said as she walked beside me.

Rebecca seemed extremely curious about Annabelle as she looked her up and down. Before Annabelle answered a loud crash rang out. I was afraid to find out what they'd done, but I knew I had to before they accidentally tore down the whole house. Kimberly was probably looking for more food. Rebecca looked at me innocently and I knew that was another bad sign.

Black streaked across the foyer and Annabelle let out a scream. She jumped and turned toward the door. I grabbed her arm to stop her from running out the front door. Pluto meowed loudly and then began licking his paws. He looked at Annabelle like she was crazy.

"What the hell is going on in here, Hallie?" she asked, clutching her chest.

Before I answered, another crash rang out and I noticed smoke filling the parlor.

"Oh my gosh, the house is on fire," Annabelle yelled out.

I took off in a sprint across the room with Annabelle following me.

"It's just a little smoke," Rebecca said as she followed behind us.

The sound had come from the kitchen, so we ran in that direction. "Maybe we should call the fire department," Annabelle said breathlessly.

I waved my arms to fend off the smoke as I pushed forward. When I reached the kitchen, I stopped in my tracks. The other coven members were standing around with innocent looks on their faces, but that wasn't the thing that concerned me the most.

Smoke billowed out from the cauldron and floated across the room. I coughed and waved my arms through the air. The women weren't the only people in the kitchen. The room was full of men. They were handsome men who strangely enough resembled Nicolas. Where had they come from? I counted and six men were now standing in my kitchen.

"Someone has some serious explaining to do," I said, glaring at the women.

They stared at me, but no one volunteered to give me an explanation. The men were equally silent.

"What? No one can speak now?" I stared at the witches.

"What's happening, Hallie? Who are these people?" Annabelle asked.

I didn't have time to answer her at the moment. Instead I looked at Sarah for an answer. For some reason, I felt she was the only one who would tell me the truth. She looked down, then finally looked up and met my gaze.

In a soft voice, she said, "Rebecca really liked the way Nicolas looked so she decided to conjure up a few guys of her own."

My mouth dropped and Annabelle let out a little gasp.

"Well, this is a first for me, and I thought I'd been in some crazy situations in the past. This totally tops all of them... combined," I said.

I looked at Rebecca. "Why would you do something like that?"

She turned and walked away from me. Without so much as a glance back, she placed her hands on one man's chest. "They are so handsome, don't you think," she said with a purr in her voice.

I crossed my arms in front of my chest. "Rebecca, I'm shocked."

I looked at the man's face. He was good-looking, but totally devoid of any expressions or any emotion. His blue eyes were blank. Rebecca stiffened, but didn't respond.

"Who is he? What did you do to bring these men here?" I asked.

The men stared blankly. Occasionally they flexed their muscles.

She shrugged. "I just did a little magic."

I shook my head. "That answer is not good enough. You cannot come into my house and wreak havoc like this."

"They are good-looking," Annabelle whispered.

"Focus, Annabelle, focus."

She nodded. "Right."

"You have to get rid of them right away," I said in a stern voice.

Frowns were immediately displayed on the witches' faces. I could tell that I wasn't their favorite person at the moment. I'd totally spoiled their fun.

"What harm can it do if they just stay around for a little while?" Kimberly asked as she stuffed a handful of potato chips into her mouth.

Annabelle looked at me.

"She has a fast metabolism," I said.

"She's always hungry," Annabelle said.

"Do the men even speak?" I asked the women.

"Well, I don't know, you haven't given me a chance to talk with them," Rebecca said, crossing her arms in front of her chest.

I shook my head. "No way, you can't talk to them. They have to go right now. Now get over there and do your little spell and make them go away. I don't even think I want to know where they came from."

"I'd kind of like to know where they came from," Annabelle said.

Barbara snickered at Annabelle's response. This was no laughing matter. What would I do with a house full of men? Heck, I didn't even know if they were really human. After all, my mother had turned a garden gnome into my senior prom date. I reached over and poked one of the men. His muscles were hard and he was definitely flesh and bone. But the fact that he didn't react to my touch was a little unnerving. Annabelle reached out and rubbed one guy's arm too. Her eyes widened as she felt his biceps. I waved my arms to capture her attention and break the trance these good-looking specimens had put her under.

"I guess you've figured out that I cast another spell last night," I said, looking at Annabelle.

Annabelle's eyes widened even more. "You didn't. Not again. Why? Is that why they are here?"

"Yes, that's why they're here." I gestured with a tilt of my head.

"Who are they and where did they come from?" she asked.

The coven members were too busy running their hands through the handsome men's hair to pay any attention to what we were saying.

"They're from Enchantment Pointe, actually. They were the coven members back in 1785. Interestingly, they were hanged for being witches," I said casually.

Annabelle nodded. "Of course, isn't that how all witches died in the 1700s?"

Surprisingly, Annabelle hadn't immediately started freaking out when I'd given her the news. That would probably come soon though.

"They think they're here to help me," I added.

"Hallie, can I speak to you in private for just a moment?" Annabelle smiled widely at the women and nodded. "It was nice to meet you all by the way." The forced smile remained plastered on her face as she gave a little wave.

"I'll be right back, ladies. In the meantime, please get rid of the men," I warned with a wave of my finger.

CHAPTER NINE

I followed Annabelle from the kitchen into the parlor.

Annabelle crossed her arms in front of her chest and stared at me. "Hallie, after what has happened, I'm not so sure you should trust these women. You haven't exactly had good luck with reanimated spirits in the past. You should get them out of the house right away."

"I know, but I can't send them back without making sure first," I whispered as I looked back into the kitchen.

The men were still standing by the cauldron with the coven members in a circle around them. If they didn't get rid of the men soon, I'd have a huge problem on my hands.

Annabelle frowned. "That's not a good idea."

"What if the book really was trying to help me figure this out by sending these women?" I said.

Annabelle released a deep breath. "I don't know, but this makes me nervous. I just want you to be okay."

I hugged her. "I know, and I promise I'll make sure to get rid of them at the first sign of trouble. Well, trouble other than conjured hunks in my kitchen."

She stared for a moment, then nodded. "Okay, if you promise."

"I promise." I crossed my index finger over my heart. I paused, then said, "That isn't all of it."

"Should I sit down for the rest?" she asked, motioning toward the chair.

"I doubt it. This couldn't be any worse than what I've already told you," I said.

"So what is it?" she asked.

"Liam called and said there is a reanimated spirit at the plantation," I said in a hurry.

"My gosh, Hallie, they're popping up everywhere. Who is this person?" she asked with a worried frown on her face.

"Liam said it was another coven member," I said.

"So one of them was just lost and went there instead?" Annabelle asked. "I guess that's an understandable mistake."

I shook my head. "No, that's not it at all. She's from 1985, not 1785."

Annabelle's eyes widened. "What? That's crazy. What did he say about her?"

"Not much else, but he's bringing her here so that I can meet her," I said.

"Well, this should be interesting. I can't wait to see what happens," Annabelle said with a cluck of her tongue.

Now I was a novelty act for everyone. "I guess they'll be here later."

"Have you told your mother yet?" she asked.

"No, I haven't been by the shop yet, but we should go there soon." My mother owned a shop in town. She concocted the best beauty potions for miles around. "I should also ask the other coven members about these women. The current coven has some history books and should be able to tell me more about these witches. Maybe then I'll know if the women really are being honest." Annabelle nodded. "Where's Jon, by the way?" I asked.

"Oh, he's outside." She motioned over her shoulder. "There was some man out there when we pulled up and he was talking with him."

I frowned. "A man? Are you sure it wasn't Nicolas? He said he was going for a walk."

"Don't you think I'd recognize Nicolas if I saw him?" she asked with a frown.

"Yes, I do, but I thought maybe you saw him from a distance," I said.

She shook her head. "No, I saw him up close."

"I don't know who he could be talking to. I don't like the sound of this though." I walked over to the tall windows lining the wall across from us.

Sure enough, Jon was outside speaking with a man. They stood beside Jon's car.

"Come on. We should go see what they're talking about," I said, motioning over my shoulder.

Annabelle followed me. After we'd made it halfway across the room, Rebecca called out, "Is everything okay?"

When I turned around, I saw the women standing at the threshold of the kitchen door. I knew without asking that they had been eavesdropping.

I plastered on a fake smile. "Off course. We're just stepping outside for a moment. We'll be right back. Why don't you all get rid of the men, then enjoy the rest of the cupcakes."

What was left of the cupcakes—all I saw was empty wrappers and crumbs, even the icing had been licked from the plate.

Their eyes lit up. "That's a good idea," Kimberly said.

The women hurried out of the foyer toward the kitchen. Their skirts made rustling sound as they rushed toward the back of the manor. The lace-up boots echoed against the hardwood floor; it sounded like a stampede.

"Remind me to tell you about their dining habits," I said as Annabelle and I walked out the front door.

When we approached Jon, he had an odd look on his face, as if he'd been caught in a criminal act and I was the police getting ready to arrest him. He looked around as if he was trying to find a location to hide the evidence, only I didn't see any evidence—other than the strange man beside him. The man wore jeans and a sweater the same shade of black as his hair. Again, I was probably just being paranoid, but with everything that had happened, it was no surprise that I was on guard. I had to be.

I looked at the man and smiled. "Hello."

He nodded and looked me up and down. Without saying a word, he turned and climbed behind the wheel of his car and turned the ignition. He looked over at us again, but then wheeled the car around and pulled down the driveway.

"Who was that?" Annabelle asked.

"He's just a friend of mine," Jon said casually.

I scowled. I wasn't buying that story. What was his friend doing at LaVeau Manor? According to Annabelle, the man had been there when they pulled up.

"Why was he here?" I motioned toward the driveway with a tilt of my head. I wasn't going to let him get away without answering that question.

Jon shrugged and shoved his hands into his pockets. "Oh, he was looking for me. I told him to meet me here since he was in the area."

Okay, I guess that could have been a truthful explanation. But why hadn't he mentioned it to Annabelle?

CHAPTER TEN

I'd left Annabelle and Jon on the veranda so that they could talk. I hoped that Annabelle would push Jon for more information about the man. Thank goodness when I stepped into the kitchen the men were gone. Just as I hadn't wanted to know exactly where they'd come from, I didn't want to know where they'd gone either.

"We got rid of them," Sarah said as she licked icing off her face.

Where had she found the icing? Had she found the extra I'd stashed in the refrigerator?

Again the other coven members frowned. They weren't happy with me and the feeling was mutual. I'd taken away their playthings. Luckily, the smoke had settled, but there was still a high magical charge in the air, and I knew exactly what was causing the feeling.

The men might have been gone, but the bad thing now was the women were at the magic again. Rebecca was trying to hide the spell by standing in front of the cauldron. I stepped closer and she attempted to block me. Guilt was all over their faces.

"Hallie, is everything okay in there?" Annabelle called out from the parlor.

I turned around to answer her. "I'll be there in a second."

When I turned back around to face the women, I realized that their current spell was just as ridiculous as the first. I stared in shock at the women, but it was like peering into the mirror. Well, almost... they were all dressed exactly like me—the same jeans, the same sweater, and even the same shoes in the same color. In the split second that I'd turned my back, their spell had taken effect and now I was seeing the results of their handiwork.

"What exactly do you think you're doing?" I asked, placing my hands on my hips.

They stared at me as if they had no clue what I was talking about.

"Well? I'm waiting for an explanation." I tapped my foot.

"We don't know what you mean," Barbara said, avoiding my stare.

"I mean, why are you all dressed like me?"

"Rebecca liked your outfit and thought it would be a good idea to conjure up a mirror image of it for all of us. I mean, we weren't exactly wearing the appropriate clothing for this time period." Barbara pulled at her jeans; clearly she'd gotten a size too big.

"It wasn't my idea alone," Rebecca huffed.

"Did you ever think about wearing something different from me?" I crossed my arms in front of my chest.

Before they had time to answer, Annabelle walked up behind me. When she reached the kitchen's entrance and saw the women, she gasped, then started snickering.

In a small way, this situation was humorous. I bit back laughter because I didn't want the women to think their behavior was acceptable. They couldn't just go around doing any spell they wanted without consequences. The fact that they liked my outfit was sweet, and I wasn't exactly a fashion plate or anything, but couldn't they have at least picked out different colors? It was like looking in a funhouse mirror. I was just glad that they hadn't taken on my physical appearance, because that would have been totally creepy. But that would probably be next.

"Hallie, I have to say this is hilarious." Annabelle snickered again.

I rolled my eyes. She might not find it so funny if the coven members were doing crazy spells in *her* house. It wasn't that they'd dressed like me—it was the fact that they wouldn't stop the witchcraft. They were out of control. Like a bunch of teenagers whose parents had left them alone for the weekend and now they were having one hell of a party.

Barbara was inspecting her shoes and Rebecca was straightening her sweater. Annabelle chuckled again. "You can't walk around like that," I said, looking at each woman.

"But it's the latest style, isn't it?" Sarah touched her arm, rubbing the sweater.

Annabelle nodded and pointed at my sweater. "Yes, as a matter of fact, Hallie just bought that sweater at the mall a few weeks ago."

"You should have gotten it in a more neutral color," Rebecca said.

Annabelle laughed again.

"Well, you could have chosen a different color on your own," I said sarcastically.

"I don't understand. If you like the outfit well enough to wear it, then why can't we have an outfit just like it?" Rebecca asked.

"Oh, you can wear the outfit all you want, just not when I'm wearing the same thing. Got it?" I asked with my arms folded in front of my chest.

"Don't we look good?" Barbara asked as she spun around.

"You all look fantastic, but as a group, we look ridiculous." I motioned around the room.

They scoffed.

"Listen, ladies, it's not the outfit." I pointed at their clothing.

"It sure sounds like it's the outfit," Rebecca said under her breath.

I glared, then said, "It's the fact that your magic is out of control. First it's the men, and now you're doing crazy things like this." I pointed at them.

"I happen to think that the men should have stayed," Barbara said.

Annabelle nodded. "They were nice to look at. Easy on the eyes."

"You're not helping." I frowned.

"Sorry," she whispered.

"You just don't want us to have any fun," Rebecca's voice went up a level.

"Have all the fun you want, just don't do any magic," I warned with a wave of my hand.

"No magic!" they said in unison.

"What do you expect us to do if we don't do magic?" Rebecca glared at me.

"There's plenty to do." I gestured around the room.

"You can read a book, or watch TV, or go shopping," Annabelle said enthusiastically.

"They don't have any money," I whispered.

"Oh, bad idea," she said. "Don't go shopping."

"Just whatever you do, don't do any more magic. Okay?" I stared, waiting for an answer.

They stared blankly at me, as if they couldn't believe that I would dare ask such a thing.

"This is where you agree with me." I nodded so that they would mimic my movement.

Finally, they nodded, and said, "Fine. We won't do any more magic in here."

They were probably just telling me what I wanted to hear, but there wasn't much I could do about it at the moment. "Thank you very much," I said, turning around and walking out of the kitchen.

The women looked a little disappointed when I'd left them. Their spell casting was out of control. Annabelle was still laughing as we made our way out to the parlor.

We'd just settled onto the sofa when Jon and Nicolas emerged through the door. Nicolas looked as handsome as ever. Jon ran his hand through his blond hair. He looked out of sorts, as if his mind was on something else. I couldn't help but suspect that it had something to do with the strange man.

Annabelle pushed to her feet. "We'd better go. I'll call you."

Jon looked at me on his way out. He looked as if he wanted to say something, but he followed Annabelle out the door without a word. I just knew there was more to the situation with the stranger. Who was that man?

CHAPTER ELEVEN

After Annabelle and Jon left, Nicolas stepped back inside to the parlor. I looked into the kitchen to see if the women had noticed him returning. My fingers were crossed that I could keep them away from him. I didn't want him to feel uncomfortable, but it looked like there would be little way to avoid it as long as the women were hanging around.

"Are they still here?" he whispered as he looked around the room.

I motioned toward the kitchen. "Yes, they're in the kitchen, probably doing another spell that they're not supposed to."

He sat down beside me. "That bad, huh?" He squeezed my hand.

"They're kind of sweet in a weird way," I said.

"What kind of spell have they cast?" he asked.

I shook my head. "I'm not sure you want to know."

"Try me," he said, folding his arms in front of his chest.

"Well, Rebecca thinks you're easy on the eyes, so she created a bunch of guys who looked like you."

His eyes widened. "Where are they?"

"Oh, I made them send the men back," I said, pointing toward the kitchen.

"That's a relief," he said, peeking over toward the kitchen.

"Yeah, except then they cast a spell so that they were dressed just like me."

He laughed. "That is kind of sweet."

I nodded. "I know, right? But I'm still suspicious of them. I mean, I have to be on guard, you know?"

"So what else is going on?" He flashed a sexy smile.

"Well, Annabelle was just here with Jon. You know, that reminds me. He was talking to some guy outside. Annabelle said the man was here when they pulled up," I said.

Nicolas quirked a brow, but continued to listen.

"Then when I went outside, the guy didn't speak to me. He just got in his car and drove off. Isn't that really weird?"

"What did Jon say about it?" Nicolas asked.

"He said that he had told the guy to meet him here, but he never said who the man was or what they were talking about," I said.

"I'll ask him," Nicolas said, then leaned over and placed his lips on mine.

My heart sped up as I pressed my body closer to his. I was totally lost in the moment when a strange noise sounded from outside. We pulled away from the kiss and looked around.

"Do you think that was the coven?" he asked.

I stood and then walked across the room, peeking in on the women in the kitchen. They were busy making sandwiches and didn't even notice that I was looking at them. When I reached Nicolas again, the same sound came across the air.

"There it is again," I whispered.

"It sounded like it came from outside on the porch," he said.

I nodded and then we headed for the front door.

Nicolas and I stepped out onto the front porch and looked around. The air was still and I didn't see anyone or anything. I prayed that another ghost wasn't out there just waiting for a chance to ask me to reanimate them. I'd had enough of that with all the ghosts that had been hiding in the woods around LaVeau Manor. Luckily, I hadn't seen any for some time.

"It must have been a bird or something," I said, looking out across the lawn.

Just then I looked down and noticed a piece of paper on the bottom step. I walked down a couple steps, then reached down and grabbed the paper.

"What did you find?" Nicolas asked, stepping up beside me.

"I'm not sure." I unfolded the paper and stared at the symbol on it. The design was familiar and all of a sudden it hit me where I'd seen it. I showed Nicolas the paper. "It's the symbol I saw sewn on the coven members' skirts."

He studied it for a moment, then handed it back to me. "They must have dropped it."

I released a heavy sigh and ran my hand through my hair. "I guess, but something makes me feel uneasy about this. I'll ask the women if they lost it. Maybe they can tell me what it means."

The women had disappeared from the kitchen and they weren't upstairs either. This was definitely disconcerting for me. I wanted them to move on to the other dimension, but I also wanted to ask them more questions; I was torn.

Nevertheless, I'd have to wait to see if they returned soon. There was so much that I needed to accomplish, but obviously the most pressing matter was to find out if what Giovanni had said about the book was true. The reanimated coven members had been of little help, so what made me think the new coven members would be any better? But with little else to help me, I had to ask.

Annabelle and I were headed to my mother's shop. I wasn't sure how my mother would react to the coven members whom I'd conjured up. One of these days my botched spells would be just too much for her to handle.

We pulled up to her shop located in the historic section of town. Enchantment Pointe was a charming little place that was set next to the river. The dark water flowed steadily along the edges of Enchantment Pointe, increasing the energy in the already magically charged town. The historic section housed many little boutiques. A lot of them were run by other witches. There was a café, antiques shop and salon nearby.

As we stepped into Bewitching Bath and Potions Shop, the bell above the door jangled announcing our arrival. I looked around for my mother. My mother had always been obsessed with beauty products and she had a natural talent for making them too. She made all the products right there in her shop.

The space was done all in white with glass jars lining the walls on each side. A large distressed white table was in the middle of the room with more beauty items. A large bouquet of white flowers was displayed in the middle of the table. To my right were the fragrances, oils, powders and herbs and the soaps, shower gels, lotions, shampoos and conditioners were on the left. My mother hated for things to be out of order in the shop, so everything always had to be in its designated spot.

"Hello, are you here?" I called out.

My mother peeked out from behind the curtain that concealed the back storeroom. At five foot one with blonde hair, my mother and I looked a lot alike. People sometimes confused us for sisters. My mother wore the store's signature polka-dotted apron over her white sweater and black and blue jeans.

At least she had both eyebrows today. I'd forever scarred her by singeing one of them off in a minor cupcake- related spell gone wrong. She used a pencil to draw her eyebrows on, but that process wasn't without its problems. Usually after a stressful or particularly hot day, she'd end up with a missing eyebrow because she'd accidentally wiped it off. So my witchcraft had caused her some distress over the years, bless her heart. She saved money on wax treatments and tweezers though.

"Sorry, I didn't hear you come in. What's wrong?" my mother asked as she hurried from behind the curtain.

I looked at Annabelle. "How the heck does she do that?"

Annabelle shrugged her shoulders. "Hi, Annette!"

The greeting didn't distract my mother from her mission. She had a strange knack for knowing when something was wrong.

"See, I knew there was something wrong. At least you didn't try to deny it this time," my mother said with the wave of her finger.

"How do you know something's wrong?" I asked.

My mother quirked her carefully drawn-on eyebrow; she'd gotten pretty good at drawing on her eyebrows after this many years. "I can sense the distress around you. You cast a spell, didn't you? What went wrong? Oh, it's really bad this time, isn't it? Not that the other times haven't been bad, because they have been really bad. So bad that I wouldn't think it possible that you could do any magic that sucked any worse."

I scowled. "Are you finished?"

"Let me sit down for this," she said, holding her chest.

My mother didn't need to remind me that my witchcraft was lacking. I released a deep breath and braced myself to tell her about the coven members.

"Okay, you're right. There is something that I need to tell you. Something did happen last night. Well, a lot of somethings. First, a man showed up. His name is Giovanni St. Clair and he said that he's the true owner of the Book of Mystics," I said.

"What does that mean?" Her face turned white.

"It means that he believes he is the leader of the Underworld," I said.

"How is that possible? You have the book. I'd say that is pretty cut and dry." She wiped her forehead and came dangerously close to eliminating the right eyebrow.

I pointed at my mother's forehead to remind her to be careful, then said, "He said some nonsense about the true owner being able to add a spell. He said his mother added a spell to the book and Nicolas' mother never added a spell."

"And obviously you've never added a spell," my mother said, grabbing her wand and waving it over the potion she'd been concocting.

Annabelle chuckled and I scowled at both of them.

"Sorry. I couldn't help myself," Annabelle said.

I waved my hand. "Whatever. I've performed bad magic in the past, but you can't say that I haven't improved."

My mother nodded. "That's true. So what are you going to do? What can I do to help?"

I shrugged. "I guess I need to find out if what he says is true. But it's looking more and more likely. How else can I explain the fact that there really is a spell in the book that his mother added?"

My mother's eyes widened. "So there really is a spell in the book? How do you know?"

Now for the hardest part; I'd have to tell her about the coven. "Well, I don't know that his mother added it, but…"

She must have read my expression because she said, "Oh, no, there's more to this story, isn't there?"

I nodded, not wanting to look into her big blue eyes.

She sat up straighter in her seat. "Go ahead and tell me. Make it quick, like ripping off a bandage. Maybe it will be less painful that way."

Okay, I knew this wasn't a great situation, but my mother was being overly dramatic. Then again, she was always overly dramatic.

"Well, when I heard about the spell, of course I wanted to look and see if there really was a spell and see if the book would tell me anything about this man's claim. So the pages flipped and there was a spell." I tried to sound calm in the hopes that my mother would follow my lead.

"So you performed the spell," she said around a sigh.

I shrugged. "Yeah, I mean, what choice did I have?"

She rolled her eyes. Annabelle moved around the room picking up bottles of spices, but she didn't get involved in the conversation. I didn't blame her. I didn't want to be a part of the conversation either.

I lowered my voice and said, "When I cast the spell I reanimated spirits."

"Spirits?" she asked loudly. "There was more than one?"

I might as well get it over with and tell her the whole thing. No sense in dragging it out. After all, she said she wanted me to make it quick like ripping off a bandage.

"I brought back an entire coven from the 1700s," I blurted out.

My mother swayed. I'd never seen my mother change to that color, nor had I ever seen her come that close to passing out. Usually she was just being dramatic, but this time I think she really was on the brink of falling off that stool and landing face-first onto the floor. I rushed over and steadied her. Annabelle placed the jar she'd held in her hands down on the counter and rushed to my mother's side.

"I'm sorry, Mom." I fanned her.

She didn't speak for a long time and I thought I might have to call an ambulance.

Finally, she managed to sputter out, "Which coven? Where are they from and where are they now?"

71

"They are from Enchantment Pointe," I said with a little glee in my voice as if this would make her feel better.

Her eyes widened. "Enchantment Pointe?"

"Yes, Enchantment Pointe. Of course they're from the year 1785, but they're here now." I chuckled nervously.

By the glare she sent my way I knew that she failed to see the humor.

"Anyway, they did confirm to me that the book had a spell added to it, so that's something, right?" I asked.

Her lip quivered at one edge as if she was trying her best to flash a teensy grin. "Yes, that's something all right."

"Are you feeling okay now?" I asked.

She nodded. "I'll be all right. What are you going to do now?"

"I was thinking maybe I should ask the modern coven if they have any information about the history on this coven," I said.

"Well, I suppose it wouldn't hurt to ask. Of course you will have to admit that you mixed up a spell again." Worry darkened her expression.

"Can you give them a call?" I asked.

She wiped her hands on her apron. "I'll give them a call now."

As she stood to grab the phone, my mother looked down at the items that Annabelle had placed on the counter. She looked up at Annabelle. "What made you pick these items?"

On the counter were small bottles of lavender oil, vanilla, and various other herbs. Annabelle shrugged. "I don't know. It just seemed like the right thing to do."

"These are exactly the items I am putting into the spell that I'm making for this cream." My mother tapped one of the jars with her index finger.

I quirked a brow. "Wow, that's a coincidence."

Annabelle chuckled nervously. "That is strange."

"Can you figure out the next spell I'm going to do?" my mother asked.

"Oh, I doubt I can do that. This was just a fluke," Annabelle said nervously.

"Why don't you give it a try?" my mother pushed.

"I couldn't," Annabelle said with a wave of her hand.

"Okay, if you don't want to do it for me." My mother looked down, giving her pretend sad face.

I shrugged. "She does that to me all the time. You may as well do what she wants."

Annabelle sighed, then said, "I guess I can give it a shot, but I know it won't work."

"Just see what happens." My mother motioned toward Annabelle.

Annabelle cautiously moved around the room, hesitating in front of each item before finally picking it up. Once she'd gathered everything, she then brought it all back and placed it on the counter. My mother reached down and inspected each item.

My mother looked at me. "I can't believe it, but she is almost exactly right."

Annabelle shook her head. "That can't be. You're just playing games with me."

"Annabelle, how long have you known me?" my mother asked.

Annabelle looked at me and then back at my mother. "For as long as I've known Hallie."

"Then you know that I wouldn't play games with you." My mother placed her hands on her hips.

Annabelle nodded, but a look of uncertainty settled on her face.

"What does this mean?" I asked.

My mother shrugged. "I don't know. Maybe Annabelle has a natural knack for potions."

Annabelle scoffed. "That's impossible. I don't do magic. It's like Hallie says, I don't have a paranormal bone in my body."

I nodded. "I do say that."

My mother grabbed the items and began mixing the spell, then said, "I don't know. Anything is possible."

Annabelle looked out the window as if she was a million miles away, but didn't respond. I sensed that she wanted to change the subject. It was odd that she'd picked out the ingredients for the spells. I didn't have an explanation, but I knew Annabelle wanted no part of spellcasting. Well, at least that was the way Annabelle had felt in the past, and I doubted she'd change her mind any time soon.

"Anyway, we have to contact the coven," I said.

I wished I could have ignored my problem for longer, but something had to be done. It probably should have been me who called the coven, but my mother had more of a connection with them. They would give more information to her than to me.

"Right. Just give me a minute." My mother grabbed the phone and punched in the number for the coven. She walked to the back of the store in order to conceal the conversation.

I exchanged a look with Annabelle. "Can you believe her? What is she telling them? That she had nothing to do with the spell? I don't care what the coven thinks anyway."

Annabelle shrugged. "Old habits, you know? I'm sure it's hard for your mother to go against the coven after all these years."

I nodded. "Yeah, I guess that's true."

Annabelle was lost in her thoughts again. I touched Annabelle's arm. "Are you okay?"

She snapped out of it and said, "Yeah, I'm good."

After a couple minutes, my mother returned to the front of the store and pushed the phone toward me. "Misty Middleton wants to talk with you."

"Oh, great," I said, taking the phone from her hand.

"She'll hear you," my mother whispered, motioning toward the phone.

Misty and I had attended the same high school. She was the head of the Enchantment Pointe Coven. Misty had always been better at spellcasting than me, but then again, everyone was better than me. That was why I'd been the outcast of the coven. Of course Misty had been a lot nicer since I'd become the leader, but still, like Annabelle said, it was hard to get rid of such deep-rooted issues.

My mother watched intently as I spoke with Misty on the phone. After a brief conversation, I agreed to meet Misty. Not because I wanted to, but because I felt like it was necessary. Plus it would be a nice gesture on my part to keep her involved on the witchy happenings that involved Enchantment Pointe.

"Call if you need anything," my mother said.

I knew she was praying that her phone wouldn't ring—she'd never gotten used to the frantic calls from me. "I'll try my best to stay out of trouble," I said, waving over my shoulder as I headed out the door.

After I said goodbye to my mother and promised that I wouldn't get into any more trouble, Annabelle and I headed out to meet Misty. Sure, I'd promised my mother, but she knew and I knew that trouble found me—there was no way to control it. I glanced back at the shop's window. My mother smiled and waved from the window.

Misty wanted us to meet her at the Bubbling Cauldron. I didn't go to the local bar often. I'd have preferred if she'd wanted to meet at the coffee shop or the bakery, although I wasn't allowed in the bakery any more—it was a long story, but involved a tiny spellcasting mishap.

As we drove down the road headed to the bar, I spotted something that wasn't quite right. After just a couple seconds it registered with me what I was looking at.

CHAPTER TWELVE

Annabelle must have had the same thought at the same time because she said, "Hey, it's those coven members you reanimated."

Much to my chagrin, she was right. They'd taken my warning to heart, because we no longer wore matching outfits. They were strolling down the sidewalk wearing their long dresses, pointy shoes, and giant black witches' hats. They looked like a picture for a Halloween costume catalog.

Now I felt guilty. I shouldn't have complained. I mean, their spellcasting hadn't really caused any problems; I needed to let them have a little fun. After all, I wasn't their mother. I shouldn't tell them what to do. But then again, they were staying at my house. I was so torn.

"I can't let them wander around town. They'll for sure get into trouble," I said.

"What are you going to do with them?" Annabelle asked.

"I don't know... I don't know," I said as I pulled over to the side of the road.

I parked the car and we jumped out, hurrying to catch up with the women. Luckily only a few people walked up and down the sidewalk and seemed to be too busy to notice the women. They had hot dogs and giant-sized sodas in their hands. When we reached the women, I touched Rebecca on the back. She jumped and the hot dog and Big Gulp went flying from her hands.

She clutched her chest when she realized it was me. "What are you doing? You almost frightened me right out of my skirt."

Annabelle chuckled.

"I'm sorry, Rebecca, but what are you doing here? I just left you at home not long ago. How did you get here?" I asked.

"You made me lose my hot dog and it had relish on it." She frowned.

"Yeah, and it's really good," Kimberly said as she chewed.

Annabelle picked the hot dog up from the ground and then gathered the cup and lid.

"Well, I can't eat it now," Rebecca said with a pout.

"I'll buy you another hot dog," I said in frustration.

My offer made me wonder where they'd gotten the money for their purchases in the first place. But that was at the bottom of my list of things to worry about at the moment. At least I hoped it was at the bottom of my list.

"Will you buy me a hot dog too?" Kimberly asked.

I stared at her. "I think she may have a tapeworm," Annabelle said.

"Okay, hot dogs for everyone, but you all have to go back to the manor. We won't even discuss how you got here. You can tell me later. So right now just get in my car." I motioned toward my car.

They followed me back to the car, but they'd done it so easily that now I was suspicious. I'd expected that they'd put up a bigger fight than that. When I stopped beside the car, I realized it was going to be a tight fit.

"You all will have to squeeze in the backseat. One of you will have to sit on the other's lap." I gestured toward the car.

"That can't be legal," Barbara said.

"How will I wear a seatbelt?" Rebecca asked.

How did they even know about seatbelts? Had they ever been in a car?

I released a heavy sigh. "We're just going right down the street."

Rebecca crossed her arms in front of her chest. People were beginning to stare.

"Okay, we'll just walk. It's not that far." I pointed down the street.

"Do they sell hot dogs where we're going?" Kimberly asked.

"Sure, they have hot dogs." I threw my hands up in frustration.

I'd be in trouble when they found out there were no hot dogs. Maybe they could eat the pretzels at the bar.

"Good, because they are tasty." She licked her fingers.

"Annabelle, how about you drive the car down there and meet us? That way we won't have to walk so far when we come back out," I said.

I'd have to figure out how to get them back to the manor after I got out of the Bubbling Cauldron.

"Where are we going?" Rebecca asked as we headed toward the bar.

"We're going to a place to see another witch," I said over my shoulder.

When we reached the front door, they stopped and peered up at the sign. The large sign hung above the door with neon bubbles rising up out of the cauldron. I was reluctant about taking them into the bar, but with any luck they'd be on their best behavior.

"I've never been to a bar before," Sarah said with wide eyes.

I imagined there were a lot of things they'd never done before. Annabelle parked the car and joined us. She was on her cell phone, but clicked off when she approached.

"Jon is picking me up so that you will have room to drive the ladies back and they can wear seatbelts." Annabelle handed me the car keys.

"Well, isn't that so sweet of you," Barbara said.

The only problem was now I'd be alone in the car with them. That would make for an interesting ride. Nevertheless, I didn't have any other options.

I opened the bar door and motioned for the women to follow. Why was Misty here in the middle of the day? This was the place that all the witches hung out in the evenings and on the weekends. I'd rarely ever gone. It was hard being an outsider. Annabelle, the witches, and I stepped inside the space. It took some time for my eyes to adjust to the darkness. The space was quiet, with faint music playing in the background, unlike in the evenings when the music pulsed and bounced off the walls. The quiet in the room was strange and almost eerie.

As soon as we stepped into the main section of the bar, the women moved toward the dance floor. That was where the giant cauldron sat in the middle of the floor. They seemed to be mesmerized by it. The witches stood around it and stared down, watching the bubbles float up toward the ceiling. As long as they didn't start casting a spell, I'd be okay. Music played lightly in the background and the women started swaying back and forth to the melody. Their dresses moved in rhythm to the sound

Misty was at the bar with her back facing us. She hadn't heard us enter, or if she had she didn't turn around. She probably wasn't looking forward to having to deal with another one of my messes now. But it wasn't her problem now so what did she care?

A man walked up in front of her. He stood behind the bar and I recognized him right away. I didn't know his name, but I'd seen him before.

"The guy who was talking with Jon is here. What is he doing here?" I whispered, pointing to the man. He made eye contact with me and I knew that he recognized me too.

We approached Misty, but she didn't turn around until we were right up behind her. She jumped and clutched her chest. "Oh, I didn't hear you all come in."

How could she not have heard us? There was little noise in the place other than the faint music playing over the speakers, and I was pretty sure our shoes were loud against the floor, especially the witches' boots. I noticed a glass with liquor in front of her. I looked at the bartender.

"I remember you," I said, pointing at him.

He offered a small lopsided smile. "Yes, I was at your place. I'm sorry I drove off so quickly. I was in a terrible hurry."

I looked him up and down. "Do you work here?"

He nodded. "Yes, I'm the new bartender."

"What is your name?" If he wasn't going to offer the information, then I'd just have to ask.

He looked at Misty, then said, "Kevin. My name is Kevin Wallace."

Did he have to confirm his name with Misty?

"So you live in Enchantment Pointe?" I asked.

"I do now," he said while exchanging a glance with Misty.

What was that all about? How did they know each other? I decided to continue my line of questioning.

"You're new to Enchantment Pointe. What brings you to town?"

If it seemed like I was being nosy, I didn't care. This guy had been suspicious and I wanted to know what the deal was.

"I have relatives in town and decided to move here."

"Wow, I've never known anyone who moved to Enchantment Pointe on purpose. There's not a lot of excitement here." I grinned.

"It seems nice so far," he said.

"Who are your relatives? Maybe I know them," I said.

"Oh, they just moved here not long ago, so you probably don't know them either." He wiped the bar with a towel and avoided my stare.

"How do you know Jon Santos?" I asked.

"We just met actually. He said he knew where I could get a deal on a motorcycle. I've wanted one for a long time."

I eyed him suspiciously again. If he was lying to me, I wouldn't stop until I got to the truth.

When the song stopped, the witches hurried over and joined us at the bar. "What are you drinking?" Barbara asked Misty.

Of course Misty was still a little freaked out that I'd reanimated the witches, so she stared for a long pause before answering.

"It's vodka and orange juice," she offered, twirling the stirring stick around her glass.

"Can we have a drink?" Sarah asked.

"I don't think that's such a good idea," I said.

The bartender pulled out glasses and placed them on the counter. "Oh, let the ladies have a drink. What's the worst that could happen?" he said as he poured the liquid into the glasses.

He couldn't be serious. I could think of about ten things right off the top of my head that could go wrong. The women quickly grabbed their drinks and downed them in record time.

"They're not shots!" I said. "You're supposed to take your time."

The women placed the empty glasses on the counter.

"How about another?" Rebecca asked.

I shook my head. "No way. One is enough."

Misty cut off the conversation. "Aren't you going to introduce me to the coven members?" She looked the women up and down.

By the expression on the witches' faces, I knew they didn't appreciate the look Misty was giving them. The witches gathered around Misty. She had a look of shock on her face.

"Are you going to eat those pretzels?" Kimberly asked.

"Um, no, go ahead," Misty said, pushing the bowl of snacks toward Kimberly.

"Who are you?" Rebecca looked Misty up and down.

"What are you doing here?" Barbara crossed her arms in front of her chest.

"Are you friends with Halloween?" Sarah asked quietly.

"Do you have any other snacks?" Kimberly waved the empty bowl that had contained pretzels through the air.

They were bombarding Misty with questions and it looked as if she might run away at any second. I'd make her squirm for a few more moments, then rescue her.

"Do you mind if we copy your outfit?" Rebecca pointed.

"I want her hair." Barbara reached out and touched a strand of Misty's hair.

At that moment it looked as if Misty might cry, so I decided to break it up.

"Ladies, please don't overwhelm Misty with questions. I need to speak with her. You all can talk to her later. Maybe she'd like to invite you over for dinner," I said.

"Oh, I would love that," Kimberly said with glee.

Misty gave me a panicked look and I just smiled in return. She could thank me later.

With my comment, Misty said, "So I hear that you have a little problem?"

Misty seemed like she was happy about that, probably because she truly was happy about my dilemma. I knew she liked that I was a screwup. But I was the leader now and that was all that mattered. But for how long would I be the leader? This problem with Giovanni was probably exactly what she wanted. She was secretly happy that I was about to lose the title.

"As you know, this coven is from the 1700s." I gestured toward the women.

I looked at the bartender. His eyes widened, but he pretended that he was working on something.

I had to get the ladies away so that I could ask Misty more questions privately. "Annabelle, could you show the ladies the pictures on the wall over there? There are a lot of witches from over the years." I pointed with a wink.

Annabelle nodded. "Let's go, ladies, you're going to love this."

The witches marched off with Annabelle. Actually, they kind of danced off with their weird interpretation of modern dance moves, instead of walking away.

"Now that they're gone, what can you tell me about the history on this coven? I have to know why they've shown up now. It had to have a meaning," I said.

Misty shrugged. "Well, if you want to know more about them I think there is a book that can tell you about the coven."

"Where do I find this book?" I asked eagerly.

The witches seemed to be growing bored with Annabelle's tour of the bar. I was running out of time.

"It's at the library, but it's in a special section. The magical section," she said in a lowered tone as if someone would hear us.

I stared at her. "There's a magical section at the library?"

"Yeah, didn't you know that?" She stared at me for a moment, then took another sip of her drink.

What else did I not know about this town? How much had they kept from me? I'd been excluded from too much.

"I never knew there was a special section," I said.

"Well, I'm sure the librarian will let you in since you are the leader now," she said with a wave of her hand.

"Gee, that's really kind of her," I said with sarcasm.

Misty rolled her eyes.

"So everyone has this special collection of books and I'd never known about it?" I asked.

She shrugged. "I just figured everyone knew."

I shook my head. "No, everyone didn't know. I didn't know."

Misty dismissed my outrage with a wave of her wrist. "Well, anyway. It had a lot about the coven from back then."

When I spotted the witches heading back my way, I said in a hurry, "Thanks for the info, Misty."

Annabelle frowned and mouthed, "Sorry."

I'd known she wouldn't be able to keep them away for long. But I'd gotten more information from Misty that I thought she'd provide, so it didn't matter.

I looked down at the empty glass in front of her, hoping she would offer an explanation. I'd known her for a long time and she'd never been much of a drinker, but if she wanted to have a drink that was none of my business. I loved enjoying a mimosa with brunch occasionally. But something seemed off about this situation and I had to know who this new man in town was.

"Thanks again, Misty," I said with a wave.

She gestured at the bartender to fill her empty glass, then looked at me. "I'll talk to you soon." Misty immediately returned her attention to the bartender. He cast a look my way for a split second, but looked away quickly when he realized I was looking at him as well.

We filed out of the bar and started down the sidewalk.

"Are we getting that hot dog now?" Kimberly asked.

It looked as if I'd better find some snacks right away. "I promise we'll get food," I said.

"Jon should be here soon. You all can go ahead and get the hot dogs if you want," Annabelle said.

I shook my head. "I don't want to leave you until Jon is here."

Before Annabelle had a chance to respond, I noticed the women had started to walk in the opposite direction.

"Oh, they're getting away," Annabelle said.

CHAPTER THIRTEEN

I ran toward the women. "I had no idea they could run so fast," I said breathlessly.

I'd almost reached them, but as I stretched my hand out to grab Sarah I stumbled and fell to the sidewalk.

"Are you okay?" Annabelle asked as she reached down to help me up.

I looked up and saw that the women had already made it out of sight. "Did you see where they went?" I asked as I righted myself.

"They walked into the diner." Annabelle pointed.

After I scrambled to my feet, we hurried the rest of the way to the diner. When I peered in through the big windows, I spotted the witches. They were in the middle of the room, looking around as if they were lost. A waitress was walking toward them. I had no idea what had possessed them to head into the diner. I mean, I assumed it was because of the food, but I didn't think they'd even known the restaurant was there. They must have smelled the French fries. They'd stop at nothing in the pursuit of a hot dog overloaded with relish and mustard.

Annabelle and I rushed through the door. No one paid the least bit of attention to us though. They were more focused on the witches with their pointy hats. The only time anyone dressed like that was for Halloween. And there were no Halloween parties today. People stared as the women walked across the dining room floor. I rushed around a few tables trying to catch up with the women before they did something that I'd have to pay for with a ton of cash. They stepped up to the counter and sat on the stools, then grabbed menus.

Kimberly took a couple French fries from a man's plate. He glared at her, but didn't say anything.

"What are you all doing?" I asked when I finally caught up with them.

They swirled around on the stools and looked at me.

"Oh hello, Halloween. Do you want something to eat too?" Rebecca asked.

I shook my head. "We don't have time to eat."

"But you said that we would get something to eat," Barbara said with a pout.

"You did say that." Rebecca wiggled her finger in my direction.

"I didn't mean right this very second. I have other things to do right now." I motioned for them to get up.

"But we are hungry now." Rebecca pulled the menu up over her face, ignoring my stare.

"Oh, look, they have hot dogs on the menu," Kimberly said with enthusiasm.

"The grilled cheese is really good too," Annabelle said.

I looked at her.

"Sorry, but it is good."

So it was the best grilled cheese ever, but that wasn't important at the moment. Apparently, there was no way they were leaving without eating. So I either had to wait for them to get food, or leave them there. Leaving them wasn't the best idea, so it looked as if we'd be placing an order. I glanced over my shoulder and saw that most everyone was still watching us.

"Okay, y'all need to order something so we can get out of here." I gestured toward the menus.

The waitress approached and asked if we were ready to place our orders. I'd fully expected for the witches to order hot dogs, but they surprised me with the grilled cheese. I was busy helping Sarah with her decision on soft drink selection and unfortunately hadn't noticed Kimberly walk away.

A piercing noise echoed across the room when the plates crashed to the ground. That was when I looked up and spotted her in the kitchen.

"What the hell are you doing?" I asked as I rushed back toward the kitchen.

"I used to cook a lot so I thought I'd see what the kitchen was like here," she said, picking up a pan.

"I think it's like any other kitchen. And you need to get out of here. They have codes and stuff and I'm pretty sure we are breaking a lot of them."

The cook was standing near the grill with a spatula in his hand, speechless. I bet he'd never had a witch storm into his kitchen before. I hurried Kimberly back to her seat and then I handed the waitress behind the counter the cash for the orders. It took way too long for the sandwiches and fries to finish, probably because we'd distracted the cook. When the waitress sat the bags on the counters, I scooped them up before the women had a chance to dig in.

"What are you doing?" Rebecca asked.

"I'm holding on to the food so I can get you all out of here and back to the manor." I nodded at a few people on our way out, trying to act as if everything was perfectly normal.

The witches followed me for the food. They could have easily knocked me down and taken off with the food. I was just glad that they hadn't figured that out yet. I walked behind the women to make sure they didn't try anything else.

"We can't wait until we get all the way back to the manor," Kimberly said as she walked along beside me.

"You can't eat in my car. It's the law," I said.

Soon enough they'd figure out that wasn't true either.

CHAPTER FOURTEEN

When we'd made it halfway back to the car, a loud noise sounded from what I assumed was the side of the building. Annabelle and I exchanged a look.

"What do you think that was?" she asked.

I shook my head. "I don't know. Maybe a cat in the trash can."

The loud boom rang out again and I was sure it had come from the same direction as the first. The witches huddled together, but continued to walk with us.

"Let's check it out," I said.

"Are you sure that's a good idea? What if it's a rat?" Annabelle shivered.

"With a noise that loud it would have to be a large rat," I said.

"That's what I'm afraid of," Annabelle said with a frown.

"I hate rats," Barbara said with a shudder.

The witches continued to follow us as we made our way over to the side of the red-brick building. When I peeked around the corner, I spotted Kevin Wallace standing in the alleyway. Only his back was visible to us as he stood behind the Dumpster, but I could still see enough of him to know it was the bartender. It seemed as though he was trying to hide, but doing a bad job of it.

"What's he doing back there?" Sarah whispered.

I shook my head, but didn't answer. Honestly, I had no idea.

He waved his arms through the air, then gestured toward the ground. Just as his arms pointed downward, another loud boom rang out.

"What is he doing?" Annabelle asked.

When I glanced over, I noticed her shocked expression. She still wasn't comfortable with the paranormal being all around her.

"I guess he's casting a spell. Let's step back a little so that he doesn't see us," I said, motioning for her to join me.

We peeked out from the corner of the building and watched as he continued his spellcasting. Magic zipped through the air and whirled around us.

"Wow, do you feel that, Hallie?" Annabelle asked.

"Yeah, whatever he's doing is powerful," I whispered.

Kevin was so consumed in what he was doing that I probably could have yelled at him and he wouldn't have noticed.

"I wonder what made him come outside and immediately start casting a spell," I said.

"That is kind of odd." Annabelle nodded.

"It's definitely odd."

I glanced over and noticed that the witches had turned back. They looked as if they were walking to my car, but I couldn't trust them.

"How will you find out what he's doing?" Annabelle asked.

"Well, I could ask him, but I doubt he'll be truthful. I'll have to think about it for a while."

It was a little creepy watching him. But just as the thought popped into my head, he stopped and turned around. Annabelle let out a little gasp. I reached for her arm and pulled her back. I knew it was too late, he had to have seen us.

"Do you think he saw us?" Annabelle asked.

I nodded. "Yeah, I'm sure he did. He was looking right at us."

"That's what I was afraid of. We should get out of here," Annabelle said.

"Yeah, we should get out of here. We have to catch the witches anyway." My heart hammered in my chest as I peeked around the side of the building again.

Kevin glared at us. Our eyes met, so I knew there was no denying that we'd been watching him. He knew I was the leader of the Underworld, so why was I worried if he knew anyway? But there was something intimidating about him.

"I think it's definitely time for us to get out of here," I said, pulling on Annabelle's arm.

"You don't have to tell me twice," she said as she took off in a sprint toward the car.

Sure enough, the witches were waiting by the car. At least they hadn't headed off for the diner. Regardless, I was glad that they hadn't made things more difficult for me at the moment.

"We have to get in the car," I yelled.

"We can't fit," Rebecca said.

"We'll have to squeeze in," I said.

I rushed around and climbed behind the wheel. The witches were smashed into the back seat. All I saw from the rear-view mirror were the giant black hats. Just as I cranked the engine, Kevin made it to the edge of the building. He looked around, but quickly spotted us.

"Hurry up," Annabelle said in a panic.

Why was I running away from this guy? I should ask him what the hell he was doing, but then again, he was rather large and I didn't want to get pulverized, so I decided leaving was the safest bet. After all, Annabelle and the witches were with me, and I didn't want to put them in danger.

As we pulled away, Kevin appeared in front of the car. I slammed on the brakes to keep from running over him.

"Keep going," Annabelle said.

Kevin walked toward us, then stopped right in front. He leaned down and placed his hands on the hood of the car.

The witches screamed and Annabelle let out another little shriek.

"What the hell is he doing?" she asked.

"What do you want?" I yelled.

He didn't take his eyes off me.

"Punch the gas," Annabelle urged.

"Run over him," Sarah said, which was totally out of character for her.

"I can't run over him."

"Why not? He's obviously trying to kill us," Annabelle said.

"Maybe something is wrong with him. He kind of looks a little out of it." My hands had a death grip on the steering wheel as I stared at him.

"That's no excuse for scaring us," Annabelle said.

"He's the devil," Rebecca yelled.

Kevin moved to his right and started around the side of my car.

"He's going to the door. Use some of your magic and zap him away," Annabelle said.

"You do remember that my magic is spotty at best, right?"

"Well, it's all we've got at the moment, unless the witches in the backseat want to whip up something."

"No way. Don't even think about it," I warned the witches.

When Kevin reached the window, he knocked on it and smiled.

Annabelle waved her hands. "Oh, no way, don't roll down the window. I don't trust him."

"Just try to stay calm. I have to talk with him. I'm the leader, remember?"

She swallowed hard and nodded. I cracked the window just enough so that I could speak with him.

"Sorry, I hope I didn't scare you, ladies," he said with a toothy grin.

"Well, you did a little. Why are you standing in front of the car?" I asked.

He smiled wider. "I thought you were having car trouble. Do you need any help?"

Something was strange about that statement. He knew that we weren't having car trouble. I didn't trust this guy. His excuse didn't add up.

"My car is fine, thank you," I said.

He stared at me for a moment longer then nodded. "I guess you were wondering what I was doing over there."

I hesitated, then said, "Yes, I was wondering a little. That was some powerful magic you used."

He nodded. "Sometimes I get a little carried away. It was just a simple spell for a good day at work. I need the tips, you know. I got bills to pay."

I nodded. "Yes, I understand." I stared for a moment longer, then said, "Well, we'd better go, I have an important appointment."

Kevin stepped away from the car and gave a little wave.

As we pulled away, I said to Annabelle, "You have to find out from Jon who that guy is."

"Oh, I plan on it. He was a scary, huh?" Annabelle said.

"I told you, he's the devil," Rebecca repeated.

CHAPTER FIFTEEN

After circling the block, I dropped Annabelle off at Jon's car. She was going to question him about Kevin while I drove the coven members back to LaVeau Manor. There was no way I was taking the witches to the library. The information I found might concern them and I didn't want the women around when I found out. I didn't know if they were just really bad at magic, or if they had more sinister motivations.

I pulled up in front of the manor, but didn't cut the engine. "Okay, ladies, please behave while I'm gone."

"Where are you going?" Kimberly asked.

"I have a few errands to run," I said.

The women eyed me suspiciously. I tried to avoid the stares as I played with the temperature control on the car.

"She's lying to us. She's doing something she doesn't want us to know about," Barbara said.

I waved off her comment. "I told you I have errands. It has nothing to do with you all."

They climbed out of the car. Rebecca turned to face me and placed her hands on her hips. "Just remember, if we find out you are lying to us, we will be most unhappy."

Our eyes met for a moment, then I pulled off in a hurry to avoid more scrutiny. I had to get rid of them. I headed over to pick up Annabelle again. She'd wanted to see this part of the library, although I wasn't sure that non-magical people could look at the books.

After that Annabelle and I would have just enough time to go by the library before Liam got there.

"How did you manage to get away without the coven members tagging along?" Annabelle asked when she slid into the passenger seat.

"I told them to make up a batch of cupcakes and where to find my cookbooks. They were delighted with the idea of little cakes as they called them. I just hope they don't burn the place down," I said as I navigated the streets of downtown Enchantment Pointe. "What did you find out from Jon?" I asked.

Annabelle shrugged. "He said he just met the guy and doesn't know him well."

"That's it? Is that all he said?"

"He acted like it was no big deal."

It looked like I would have to question him myself. This was definitely a big deal.

"Maybe the guy is harmless, but I don't want to take any chances," I said.

We drove in silence for a moment, then Annabelle asked, "Do you miss Liam?"

I navigated the road toward the library, but didn't look over at her. I knew she was staring—I felt her eyes on me.

"I don't know what to think. Yes, I miss him, but right now things are going well with Nicolas."

I finally glanced over. Annabelle nodded. She understood completely. At least someone got me.

We pulled up to the library and I wheeled in to the first available parking spot. I had to admit that I was a bit skeptical about what I would find. A secret section for witch information? That was ridiculous.

Annabelle and I hurried across the parking lot and into the library. It was a large building. Well, large for Enchantment Pointe. We'd been lucky and had a donation from an Enchantment Pointe resident, so now we could enjoy this beautiful restored library.

I looked around the room. Tables with library lamps lined the floor to my right with stacks behind that. The large reference desk was to the left and more stacks were in front of us. I had no idea where this special secret section was though. If Misty was playing a trick on me I would be extremely angry.

Of course the space was silent and I didn't see anyone—no patrons, not even the librarian.

"Where is everyone?" Annabelle whispered.

"I don't know, but it's spooky in here," I said as I stepped a little further into the space.

Just then the librarian poked her head around one of the stacks. I hadn't expected for her to have pink streaks through her hair. She definitely had broken the stereotypical librarian image that came to mind.

"Oh, hello. I didn't know anyone was here. What can I do for you?" She looked me up and down as she adjusted her eyeglasses. "Oh, I know you. You're Halloween LaVeau. I'm sorry to hear about your great-aunt. How do you like living at LaVeau Manor?"

I smiled. "It's lovely and I'm enjoying it very much." There was no need to burden her with all the little details of what it was truly like living at LaVeau Manor.

"I have photos of the home from the early 1800s if you'd like to see them sometime," she said as she walked over to us.

"I'd love that. Thank you," I said.

"Is there anything else I can help you with?" she asked as she looked from me to Annabelle.

I looked around, then said, "I was told that you have a special… um, a special section on witches and the witchcraft in Enchantment Pointe."

I don't know why I felt weird asking her about this. She obviously knew I was a witch. But the fact that I hadn't heard about this selection of books made me not too excited about asking a stranger about this secret section.

She nodded and glanced at Annabelle. "It's down in the basement, but only witches are allowed in the room. Follow me."

I frowned. I wasn't sure I wanted to go into this place alone. Especially since I found out it was in the basement. Sure, stick me down in the creepy basement all alone. There were rumors that the place was haunted. That was the last thing I needed—more ghosts.

"Here's the room." She gestured as she opened the basement door.

"I'll just wait upstairs," Annabelle said, rubbing her arms and looking around the dimly lit space.

I frowned. I shouldn't have been surprised since we all knew that Annabelle didn't deal well with the paranormal or any creepy situation for that matter. I wondered if part of Annabelle's aversion was her unwillingness to deal with the growing suspicion that she actually might have some paranormal skills.

The librarian's eyes widened as if she didn't want to hang around the basement either. She stepped away from the door and motioned for me to enter. "Let me know if I can help."

By the way she was distancing herself from the basement door, I wasn't sure if she was sincere about her offer. She turned to walk away before I'd even had a chance to reply.

"Well, there is one thing you can help with." I rushed my words before she had time to get away.

"What's that?" she asked, looking over her shoulder.

"I'm looking for a book that has information about the witch coven from 1785."

She twisted her hands nervously, then said, "The years are marked on the shelves. You should be able to find all the information you need on that year."

I nodded. "Thanks."

I hesitated and looked back as Annabelle followed the librarian up down the hall. It was just me now. Or maybe the ghost I'd often heard about. I inched my way down the steps. Overhead fluorescent lights blinked and buzzed at the back of the room. Couldn't they have replaced the bulbs?

On my right was a room. Oddly enough, the door was clearly marked with the word 'Witchcraft.' I stepped into the cramped pea-green-colored room and looked around at the books. How would I find the specific one I was looking for among the crowded shelves? The librarian had been right; the years were marked on the top of each shelf. But I had no idea what to expect.

It was a strange collection. One thing I noticed right away was that the books only went back to 1785—the year the coven members claimed they'd died. That was odd. I stepped over to the section and scanned the spines lining the shelf. Each book had a different topic—one for spells, one for rules of witchcraft, even one for hiding witchcraft. Of course these weren't original books from the 1700s, but it would be fascinating to read about what was going on back then.

Finally, I reached a book with the title *Enchantment Pointe Coven* on the spine. I grabbed the tome from the shelf and pulled out the chair next to the small table in the middle of the room. I was anxious to read what it said about the coven members. Was their magic just as bad back then?

I flipped through the pages, but none gave me much information. Just as the witches had said, they had been hanged for practicing witchcraft when their coven had been discovered. But when I turned another page, I was shocked to discover my great-great-great-grandfather's name. Rebecca had said she'd known him.

As I read the page, I soon discovered that he had been instrumental in getting the witch-hunting madness stopped, but it had been too late. He had risked his life for the women, but the women had died anyway. Maybe that explained why my great-great-great-grandfather had gone missing. The book gave a description of the women, but it didn't exactly match the women who were in my home.

The women had formed the first coven in Enchantment Pointe, although apparently there had been plenty of women and men before them practicing their magic. The formation of that first coven had been an important part of the development of Enchantment Pointe. Maybe that was why they had been called back to help me. They were there from the start, but did they have the answers I needed? On the first page I noticed the symbol that had been sewn on the witches' skirts. I had to ask them what it was for.

Unfortunately, I couldn't take the book with me. I'd have to confront the women with the information that I'd found. Whether or not I would get answers was a whole different story. None of the other spirits I had reanimated had ever been truthful with me, so I didn't expect that to change now.

After placing the book back on the shelf, I hurried out of the room and up the stairs as if something was chasing me. I didn't really think anything was chasing me, but it was the power of suggestion, right?

Annabelle was sitting at one of the tables when I returned. She was looking at the newspaper. "What did you find?" she asked as she pushed to her feet.

"Not much," I said around a sigh. "We'll head back to the manor and I'll tell you what I found."

"Sounds good. This place is creepy." She shivered again as we headed toward the door.

"Thank you for everything," I said to the librarian as we hurried out the door.

CHAPTER SIXTEEN

Annabelle and I arrived at LaVeau Manor a few minutes later. The place loomed over us as I parked the car out front. It was as if the house was saying, *It's about time you came home*. When I'd first gotten the manor I'd had no idea what I would do with it. How would I ever fill up the rooms? Now it didn't seem as if I was having a problem filling up the place. They just weren't the type of guests I'd expected.

Trees surrounded the property on both sides of the manor. A long pebble driveway led to the house and a large iron gate with stone columns stood at the end. The veranda stretched the width of the house.

The manor was three stories. On the top floor was a small window which lit the attic. I stared up at that little window and thought about how the discovery in that small space had led to all this craziness in my life. What would have happened if I'd never found the book? Something told me that wasn't possible—it was fate that I'd found the book. But now the book was being taken away from me.

The bright sun shimmered down across the landscape and white fluffy clouds dotted the endless blue sky. The day had turned slightly cooler and I was thankful for the relief from the heat. Liam would be there soon with the other witch. But for right now, I had to find the coven members. For one, to make sure they hadn't cast more spells, but most importantly, I wanted to ask them about the information from the book. I'd also ask the women about the coven member who had showed up at Liam's front door.

"It's quiet around here. It spooks me out when it's quiet like this. I need noise," Annabelle said with wide eyes.

To be honest everything spooked her out, so I didn't comment.

When we stepped inside, I noticed the same type of heavy silence that Annabelle had noted while we were outside. The only noise was from the tick-tock of the grandfather clock.

"Where are the coven members?" Annabelle asked as she eased into foyer.

I shrugged. "I don't know. Like I said, I left them in the kitchen baking more cupcakes."

Something seemed off about the place, but I couldn't put my finger on what it was exactly. The feeling was probably just anxiety about all that was going on; it was enough to cause panic attacks. I walked across the rooms and made my way to the kitchen. There was no sign of the women, but a strange feeling hung in the air; I might even say that it whirled around the room.

"Does it seem strange in here to you?" I asked Annabelle.

"It does seem a little stranger than usual. And that's saying a lot." The whisper of her voice tickled my ear. She stood behind me so closely that she was practically on my back.

"You feel that vibe too then? I'm not imagining things," I said.

"No, but it's always really weird in here so that's not saying much," Annabelle said as she looked around.

I stepped into the space, then walked over to the cauldron. It looked as if it had been used recently. What kind of spells were they casting this time? It wasn't as if I cared if they used the cauldron, but after the other spirits I'd had around, I'd lost my trust in the reanimated. Besides, I didn't want to enable their bad behavior. I touched the inside of the cauldron to see if I could figure out which herbs they'd used. But I soon realized that there were remnants of so many it would be impossible for me to know.

The doorbell rang and Annabelle jumped again, clutching her chest. I hoped that it was Nicolas or Liam. Although I'd told Nicolas he didn't have to ring the bell anymore.

"That scared the hell out of me," Annabelle said.

She followed me as I went back across the house and to the front door. I peeked out the door. Liam's handsome face was the first thing I saw. I let out a sigh of relief, but it was short-lived because I remembered that he had this random witch with him. I had no idea what to expect.

"Is that Liam? Is she with him?" Annabelle asked as she strained to look over my shoulder.

I cast a look to the right of Liam and saw the woman standing beside him. Her big brown eyes were rimmed with thick lashes. Her cheeks had a natural pink hue and her brown hair shone in the sunlight. It looked as if she'd just stepped off a retro Eighties movie set. She wore a white blouse with wide shoulder pads, electric blue stirrup pants and matching cobalt-colored plastic jelly sandals. She had a giant lace bow in her hair.

I opened the door and smiled at Liam and the woman. She didn't look anything like the other coven members, so I figured that there was no way she was a part of their coven. Based on the clothing, she had to be telling the truth about being from the 1980s.

I opened the door. "Please come in."

"It's good to see you," Liam said as he stepped close and placed a kiss on my cheek.

My heart sped up and I felt as if I'd been poked with an electrical cord. "Thanks for coming," I said softly.

"Hallie, this is Kelley Killebrew." Liam gestured toward the woman.

"Nice to meet you," she said sweetly.

I thought I detected a slight Southern accent, but I wasn't sure. Maybe as she talked more I would figure it out. Was she from around here?

"Won't you please come in? We can sit in the parlor and talk," I said, motioning across the foyer.

She nodded and smiled. "Thank you."

I looked at Annabelle. She shrugged and whispered, "How weird is that?"

"I'm getting used to it at this point," I said.

We followed Liam and Kelley into the room. The silence of the room made the sound of our footsteps echo even louder and only amplified the strangeness of this whole encounter.

"Please have a seat anywhere you'd like." I gestured.

Kelley looked around, then eased down onto the sofa. Her back was ramrod straight as she leaned back onto the cushion and her hands were placed on her lap. She sat there with a big smile on her face. I stared for a moment, not sure of what to say.

"So, like I said, Kelley showed up at the plantation and she doesn't know why she was there," Liam offered, breaking the silence.

I guessed now was the time that I had to talk to her about what I'd done.

"Kelley, do you remember anything about what happened?" I leaned forward in my chair so that I wouldn't miss a word she said.

"I remember that I was a witch with the coven here in Enchantment Pointe. I was killed in a car accident," she said softly, then looked down.

My eyes widened. "Here in Enchantment Pointe?"

Was I bringing back all former coven members from Enchantment Pointe? And if so, why? At least that answered my question about where she was from.

"I'm sorry that I accidentally called you back. It was just a spell gone wrong." I flashed a small smile. "I occasionally have problems with my spells."

Annabelle coughed. Yeah, I knew it was more than occasionally, but Kelley didn't have to know that little detail.

She waved off the apology. "I'm glad you did. This gives me a second chance to make things right."

Uh-oh. What was I going to do with this woman? And what did she mean that she wanted to make things right? What had she done wrong?

"I have a feeling that I was brought back for a reason and I plan on finding out what that reason is," she said softly.

The doorbell rang and broke up our conversation. We exchanged looks because I knew they were all wondering the same thing as me. Had another reanimated witch shown up at my doorstep?

I hurried over and peeked out the front door. Jon stood on the doorstep. He was just the man I wanted to see. Since Annabelle hadn't been able to get any real answers about the bartender, I would have to ask.

I opened the door and stepped aside so that he could enter. "Hi, Jon."

"Is Annabelle here now? I hope she didn't leave without me," he said with a smile.

"We're in the parlor." I motioned with a tilt of my head.

Jon followed me back to the room. He eyed Kelley, probably wondering where the costume party was. Annabelle jumped up and kissed Jon.

I decided not to waste any time asking Jon about Kevin. "We ran into that friend of yours," I said, watching him for a reaction.

"Which friend?" he asked casually.

"The one who was just here at LaVeau Manor. He said his name is Kevin Wallace."

His eyebrows shot up in surprise. "Really? Where did you see him?"

"Apparently he works at the Bubbling Cauldron. And he was practicing some pretty powerful magic too," I said.

"You all were at the Bubbling Cauldron?" Nicolas asked from over my shoulder.

I spun around. "I didn't hear you come in."

Nicolas kissed my cheek. "Sorry, I didn't mean to scare you. So, you were at the Bubbling Cauldron?"

I realized that it seemed a bit out of character for me to go to a bar in the middle of the day, but it wasn't that crazy. Everyone was staring at me for an answer. Annabelle flashed a sympathetic grin.

I pointed to Annabelle so they would know I hadn't been alone. "We went there to speak with Misty Middleton. She was there talking to that new guy. He claims he is new in town."

Liam and Nicolas exchanged a look.

"There's a new witch in town? That never happens," Liam said.

"What's this guy's name?" Nicolas asked.

"Kevin Wallace. But you should ask Jon, he said he knew him." I pointed toward Jon.

Jon held his hands up. "Hey, I haven't known him that long. He started talking to me the other day when I stopped in there. He seemed like a nice enough guy and I figured I would help him out since he is new in town. I told him about a guy who has a motorcycle for sale. He met me here so that I could give him the number."

"This guy might be on the up and up, but it wouldn't hurt to check him out. We don't need any more problems," Nicolas said.

"Let's go," Liam said, jumping up from the seat.

Jon looked hesitant, but he finally joined them.

"What are you going to say to the guy?" I asked Nicolas as he stopped to kiss me goodbye. Liam looked at us, but turned away and headed for the front door.

"We'll just let him know that he has to be a little more forthcoming." He touched my cheek. "We don't want vague answers."

"Do you think this could be in relation to Giovanni?" I asked.

Nicolas gave a quick nod. "Anything is possible, but we're not going to take a chance."

"Let me know what you find out," I said.

I wanted to go with the men, but I had more to do here. Namely, I needed to figure out what the newest reanimated coven member wanted and where the other coven members had disappeared to. I knew there was no way that they'd gone for good. I could never be that lucky.

Nicolas turned and walked toward the door. I hoped they got answers from Kevin. If anyone could, I knew they would. I watched from the window as Nicolas and Liam headed down the driveway.

After they disappeared from sight, it was just Annabelle, Kelley, and me. For a few seconds, we just stared at each other. I had no idea where to even start. What would I do with another coven member?

"So you are prepared to stay around then, huh?" I asked.

Kelley smiled softly. "Oh yes. I can't wait. I have a lot to do. I have to find my friends and family members, although my parents are dead. I need to talk with you about bringing them back. I mean, I'm sure you can't bring everyone back, but I'm sure you can make an exception in this situation. I noticed the clothing styles have changed. Shoulder pads are out, right?" She stared at us.

She sure did talk a lot. I felt bad that she missed her parents, but there was no way I could bring them back. I wouldn't tell her that just now though.

"Yes, the style has changed, but some Eighties fashions have made a comeback," Annabelle said.

"What about leg warmers? Can I still wear them?" Kelley looked from Annabelle back to me.

Annabelle and I shook our heads. "No, not unless you're dancing," Annabelle offered.

As much as I wanted to talk about fashion—and believe me, I did, because I hadn't been able to talk about anything normal in ages—I couldn't make the time for it right now. My status as leader was at stake.

CHAPTER SEVENTEEN

A loud bang sounded out. Annabelle and I hurried over to the foyer. The gang of coven members rushed through the front door like they were being chased by a crazed clown carrying a chainsaw.

"Where have you all been?" I crossed my arms in front of my chest. I felt like I was their mother asking why they'd been out so late.

"We've been busy exploring the outside of the manor." Rebecca motioned over her shoulder.

I eyed them all suspiciously. "Well. Okay. I guess that's okay. Did you all do anything in the house while I was gone? It looked as if you used the cauldron in the kitchen."

"Oh, was that not okay?" Rebecca asked.

"We just did a spell for beautiful weather so that we could enjoy the outside." Barbara smiled.

That seemed a little too innocent if you asked me. I furrowed my brow. "Well, considering I asked you not to do any more spells…"

Suddenly a crash rang out. The noise had come from the kitchen. We ran across the room and when I reached the kitchen, I found the cauldron had fallen onto the floor. What the heck had happened?

"Oh dear. That's unfortunate." Rebecca shook her head.

What had they done to the cauldron? That cauldron had been in my family for ages. Maybe I didn't get a lot of use out of it, but I still didn't want it destroyed.

"We'll help you lift it back up," Sarah said as she motioned for the women to join her.

With some grunting and groaning, the coven members and I lifted the cauldron back onto its hook. I wiped my hands on my pants and turned around to see that Kelley was looking at me oddly. I knew I had to explain that I had the Book of Mystics and that I'd brought back the other witches too. Surely she would know about the book if she was a coven member. If the women from 1785 knew, then she had to know of its existence too.

Had I really brought back all of the witches? The odds were likely that I had. How else would they have gotten here? Nope. There was no other way. It was definitely my fault.

"I have the Book of Mystics," I said, looking at Kelley.

She nodded. "Well, since you're the leader, I assumed that you had it. I hope everything is all right," she said with a look of concern.

So she was aware of the book. That led me to my next question. "Who was the leader when you were here last?" I asked.

She frowned. "You'll have to excuse me, but I'm not so good with names. I can't seem to remember many names since I've returned."

"Oh, I understand. I'm sorry," I said.

I hated to press her for info, especially since the poor girl was having memory issues, but any little details she could provide could possibly be of tremendous help.

"Do you remember anything about the leader? Was it a man or a woman?" I asked.

I should have been able to find this information at the library. If she couldn't remember, maybe I'd go back and take a look.

She scowled in concentration. "It was a man. Yes, it was definitely a man. I think he had dark hair and was very tall."

"Is there anything else you can remember about him?" I pushed.

Maybe I was being paranoid, but the description she'd given sounded a lot like Giovanni. I wasn't sure why he was the first one who came to mind when she'd described him.

She shook her head. "I'm sorry, but that's all I can remember about him."

I waved off her apology. "Please don't apologize. I totally understand," I said.

Annabelle gave Kelley a pitying smile.

"Maybe the name will come to me soon," Kelley offered.

There was just one more question and I promised myself that I would stop making her try to remember things.

"What happened to him?" I asked. "Was he still the leader when you died?"

She nodded. "As far I know, yes, he was still the leader."

Okay, I'd said it was the last question, and I really meant it this time. "Was there anything unusual about his time as a leader?"

"You heard the girl, she doesn't remember anything, now stop asking," Rebecca said in a frustrated tone.

I frowned. "I'm just trying to find out what I can about former leaders."

"Go to the library," Barbara said.

Annabelle and I exchanged a look. So they knew about the library? What else did they know?

Now that I knew they were aware of the library section, I decided to ask them about the strange symbol on their clothing. "As a matter of fact I've already been to the library." I folded my arms in front of my chest. They paused and stared at me. "And I found out a little about you all," I said.

"What did you discover?" Rebecca stiffened.

"Not a lot, but I did see a picture of the symbol that's on your skirts." I pointed. They looked down at their dresses. "What does it mean?" I asked.

"It helps us with our spells," Rebecca said matter-of-factly.

That was interesting. Maybe I could get this symbol to help with my magic?

I held up my index finger. "Wait here. I have something I want to show you."

I retrieved the paper I'd discovered and hurried back to the witches. I motioned for them to come closer. When the coven had gathered around, I asked, "I need to know more about this symbol?"

I showed them the paper. Rebecca picked it up and studied it, then passed it around to the other coven members. When they'd finished looking at it, they handed it back to me. I looked at them expectantly. By the looks on their faces, I was sure they had the answer to my question.

Rebecca looked at me, then said, "It looks like our symbol, but maybe it's not quite the same. Something seems different."

My mouth dropped open. "What do you mean? It's the symbol associated with your coven. I discovered it in the book I found at the library."

"We had a problem deciding on just one, so we tested quite a few," she said.

I stared in disbelief. "You should still know what each one that you thought about using means."

"Well, we can't remember all of that—after all, it's been a long time. We have good memories, but not that good."

I couldn't believe that they were that useless. "Well, can you all at least help me try to figure out this mystery?"

Rebecca shrugged, then the rest of them followed the gesture. "Sure, we can give it a try."

I loaded the women into my car and we headed to the library. The women chatted non-stop about all the things that had changed around town. They were surprisingly accepting of all the things they saw around them.

When I passed by the bakery, Kimberly leaned forward in the seat. "Can you stop off at the bakery? We are really hungry."

I looked at her in the mirror. "Are you serious? I'm kind of in a hurry."

I looked back at all the scowling faces and realized that they were completely serious. I pulled my car over and parked along the curb. I couldn't believe that I was taking a group of witches from the 1700s to the bakery. I was kind of curious as to which type of doughnut they'd pick.

Technically I still wasn't allowed in the bakery. I missed the chocolate glazed doughnuts. Unfortunately, the witches had purchased several of the scrumptious aforementioned doughnuts. After they finally got their pastries, I got the women back in the car and I hurried the rest of the way to the library.

"You need to slow down," Barbara pointed out.

"My driving is fine."

A horn honked from somewhere behind me. The ladies cackled. "That's what you think," Rebecca said.

I pulled the car into the parking lot and all the women climbed out. They still nibbled on their goodies.

"You have to finish eating before we can go inside," I warned.

I watched as the women chewed the last few bites of food, and then we walked into the library and they looked around.

Their eyes widened. "I still can't believe all the books. There are so many," Sarah whispered.

I walked across the library and motioned for the women to follow me. I wondered if they would have the same feeling about the creepy basement as I did. We reached the stairs and I hesitated.

"What's the problem?" Rebecca asked.

I shook my head. "Nothing. It's just a little weird down there," I said, pointing to the basement.

She waved her hand dismissively. "Oh, that's ridiculous. Now come on, we have other things to do today."

I snorted. "Like what? Cause more chaos around the manor?"

"That wasn't a very nice thing to say," Barbara said with a wave of her finger.

I shrugged. It was the truth though. They followed me as I led the way down into the dimly lit basement.

"I don't know what your problem is with this place. It seems fine to me," Rebecca said.

She would say that. I wasn't surprised that it didn't give her the creeps. Rebecca seemed tough as a cast-iron cauldron.

When we reached the room, I motioned for them to follow me inside. We stepped inside the space, they looked around in amazement.

"All of these books are about us?" Barbara asked.

"Well, not about you all. Just all witches from Enchantment Pointe."

She looked at me as if she was pondering this information. I got the impression that she was a little disappointed by this news. It had been quite a few years and more covens had come along since then, although witches did have a longer lifespan.

She released a sigh. "Well, I guess you can show us the book now."

I walked across the room and moved to the spot where I had found the book before. For a moment I didn't see it and I began to panic. But finally I spotted the book. It had been moved to a different spot from when I'd found it before. Had someone else been in the room? I didn't think there would be many witches researching that often. There couldn't have been too many people who would have looked at the book. I figured I had been the only one down there in this room for a long time. I pulled the book from the shelf, carried it back to the table, and placed it down in front of the witches.

I flipped open the old cover and leafed through the pages until I found the spot with the symbol. "See," I said, tapping the page. "There it is. Can you help me reverse his spells?"

The women gathered around the book and peered down. They were quiet way longer than I wanted them to be.

Finally, I had to say something. "Well, what do you think?"

Rebecca flipped the cover closed and headed toward the door. "Okay. We're ready."

"What do you mean you're ready?" I asked.

She turned around and looked at me. "We're ready to help you."

I picked the book back up and placed it back on the shelf where I'd originally found it. I hurried out of the room because the women had already left me and were moving up the stairs.

"Hey, don't leave me down here in this place," I said.

We piled back in to the car and headed for LaVeau Manor. Thank goodness they didn't ask to stop off for more pastries, although Rebecca and Kimberly did want to stop and pick up a Diet Coke. They'd become obsessed with them. Soon I'd have to stage an intervention.

Once we finally arrived back at the manor, I was exhausted just from listening to all their chatter and we hadn't even started to cast a spell yet. They claimed they could help me get rid of the spells that had been added to the Book of Mystics. I was a bit skeptical, but I could use all the help I could get, so I had to let them try.

I wasn't sure how they knew which spell would help break anything that Giovanni had done. There was some feeling deep down that told me they had no idea what they were doing. It was all so complicated, but none of this had ever been easy.

CHAPTER EIGHTEEN

We gathered around the big black cauldron. The wind whipped as the witches cast their spell. We held hands and recited the words. A white misty cloud circled our heads and then fell down to our legs. It whirled around the ground, weaving in and out between our legs, and then rose back up and hovered over our heads.

The wind died down and I hoped that we had finally finished the spell. I was drained of all energy. I wasn't sure how long I could continue. But I had to keep trying. Giving up was never an option.

The women released hands and looked up. The clouds had disappeared. "The spells should be gone from the Book of Mystics," Rebecca said.

I reached for the book and opened it to the back. The spells were still on the pages. I released a deep breath and tapped the page with my finger. "Sorry to break it to you, ladies, but the spells are still there."

A few gasps rang out from the women. Rebecca shrugged nonchalantly.

"That can't be," Barbara said, leaning over to look.

"Well, it's the truth," I said.

"I hate to break up your conversation," Rebecca said. "But Kimberly wants more food." The reanimated sure were hungry. Rebecca didn't seem too concerned that I was having a spellbook crisis at the moment.

"I don't know if I have any food left," I said.

"Maybe you should go to the store," Kimberly said.

I frowned. "Yeah, I guess I should. But I have a little matter with the Book of Mystics that I have to figure out first."

Kimberly shrugged like it was no big deal.

"Come on, I'll see what I can dig out of the pantry." I motioned over my shoulder.

As I rooted around in the cabinet looking for a leftover rice cake or a pack of forgotten saltines, Rebecca stood behind me. I'd felt her presence. When I glanced over my shoulder, I saw her standing there with her hands on her hips.

"You have more power than you realize. You should cast a spell on your own to see if a spell appears in the book. Then maybe you'll have the answer you're looking for," Rebecca said.

I doubted what she said. Besides, I wasn't sure that I wanted the answer. What if I couldn't add a spell? Would that mean that I would have to give up being the leader of the Underworld?

"Yes, dear, you should give it a try," Barbara said.

I sucked in a deep breath and said, "Fine. I'll give the spell a shot."

The women were standing around the room, patiently waiting for me to begin. I stepped over to the book on the counter and everyone gathered around.

Annabelle stood in the corner and watched. Kelley jumped right in as if she'd been around forever. Now that we'd secured the cauldron back on the hook, I opened the book and waited for something to happen. But there was no wind, no lights… nothing. It was as if the book had stage fright. The witches looked at me.

"You realize you can place a spell on the book so that no one but you can touch it?" Rebecca asked with a stern look on her face.

"If it was as easy as placing a spell, then why didn't the previous leader do that?" I asked.

"I would assume that she did, but I don't know the circumstances," she pointed out.

"If a spell to keep people away can be added, then why was the book hidden when I found it? Obviously my aunt hadn't wanted anyone to find it," I said.

"Well, she wasn't the leader of the Underworld," Rebecca said.

I supposed she did have a point there, but something still made me skeptical. Maybe it was because my magic had been bad in the past. But I supposed it was worth a shot. What was the worst thing that could happen?

"Let's hold hands and we can help you with the spell. You can use our energy." The women gathered around and held hands.

Now that wasn't such a bad idea. I'd used Nicolas and Liam's energy in the past and it had helped me pull off complicated spells.

Kelley and Annabelle watched from a distance. I didn't blame Kelley for not wanting to get involved.

I grasped the witches' hands and recited the words. They were silent as I spoke, but soon they started chanting. I had never in all my years taken part in a spell where the witches had chanted as a part of a spell that I had been trying to cast. The air changed and the temperature grew hot. Sweat beaded on my forehead. I'd never felt this way before and I knew something was wrong.

Without warning, a ring of fire encircled the book and it inched its way closer to the vulnerable pages. I leapt forward and reached past the flames, grabbing the book. I fell backward with the book clutched in my arms. Gasps rang out and the witches jumped forward with towels, patting out the flames.

After the fire was out, I looked at them. "What the hell was that all about?"

Rebecca had a sheepish look on her face. "Oops. I guess we got a little carried away."

A little carried away? That was an understatement. "You almost caught the book on fire." They were a walking disaster.

Kelley walked over and helped me to my feet. "Are you okay? That was scary."

I nodded and brushed the hair out of my eyes. "Yes, I think I'm fine." I looked down at the book. Thank goodness the flames hadn't touched it and it was perfectly fine. What would I have done if I'd allowed them to destroy the book? What would happen to the Underworld? It would be chaos. But after all the madness, had the spell to protect the book really worked?

Kelley must have read my mind because she asked, "Did the spell work?"

I released a deep breath. "I don't know."

"May I try to touch the book? That way you'll know if it worked."

I looked at her reluctantly.

"Come on, what would I do with the book if I tried to take it from you? You and your friend would tackle me and have it back within two seconds."

Yeah, but what if she tried a spell and took the book that way? Then again, if she wanted to do that she wouldn't need me to hand it to her, right? The more I thought about it the more confused I got. She grinned with that sweet face and I suddenly felt as if I could trust her. I handed her the book.

Unfortunately, she was able to take it from my outstretched hand. Fortunately, my instinct had been correct and she handed it back to me with a smile.

"Try to do another spell," Barbara said.

The bell rang and we all jumped. It was just as well that someone was at the door and had stopped me because the spells weren't working anyway.

"I'll get the door." I grabbed the book, because I'd learned the hard way that I couldn't trust anyone.

If Nicolas and Liam had gone to the Bubbling Cauldron, then who was at my door?

When I reached the door, I peered out and cursed when I saw who was standing on the veranda. I reluctantly opened the door. Giovanni gave a sneering grin and looked down at the book clutched under my arm.

"I see that you've brought the book to me." His mouth twisted into a wicked grin.

"Are you crazy?" I snapped.

He looked offended that I would ask such a question, but he didn't answer.

"No, I didn't bring you the book. What do you want?" I demanded.

"I've come for the book of course." His voice dripped with mockery.

"Well, that's not happening," I said.

"Why doesn't he add a spell if that's what he claims he can do?" Kelley said from over my shoulder.

I looked back and everyone was standing behind me. Annabelle shrugged. Rebecca was proposing a risky situation. Was I willing to give it a try? What would I do if he really could add a spell? Would I have to give him the book?

I reluctantly allowed Giovanni into my home. Of course I followed him as he stepped into the kitchen. I didn't trust that he wouldn't make a wrong move. The book was still on the counter. I stood nearby because I didn't trust him not to grab it and run away. I'd hate to zap him with magic, but I would if I had to. I never liked using magic against anyone and I'd only do it if absolutely necessary.

He smiled at the group of witches, then began reciting the words. He waved his hands and the wind whipped. I'd never seen anyone do magic that aggressively before. I was positive that he had no idea what he was doing.

The wind wasn't as strong as when I performed magic and I felt a little self-satisfied about that little fact. When the wind finally settled down, he opened his eyes and looked around the room.

"Well, have a look, ladies." He gestured with a grand sweep of his hand.

I peered down at the book and sure enough, the spell that he'd just performed had been added to the pages. I was devastated. What would I do now? There was no way around it. He had added a spell and I had not. It looked like he had won this match. Giovanni met my gaze and my stomach turned when I saw the look of satisfaction on his face.

Giovanni reached down and grabbed for the book. I snatched it up, but fell back onto the floor.

"Not so fast," I said as I sat on the floor.

"The book is mine. I added the spell and you did not. There is no way around this now, Halloween LaVeau. So be a nice little witch and give me the book." He wiggled his fingers.

I looked around the room at the faces staring at me.

"It does appear that it is his book now," Rebecca said.

The rest of the coven members nodded. Annabelle reached down and helped me to my feet. There was no way I would let him have the book without a fight. I needed time to confirm what he had said. I didn't care what he'd added to the pages.

Giovanni stepped forward and I moved back a few steps. Annabelle stood beside me, holding on to my arms as we moved together. He had us backed into a corner. There was nowhere else to go. There was nowhere to get away from him. Maybe if Annabelle moved across the room, I could toss it to her.

In one swift movement, Annabelle reached down and grabbed the book. I let out a gasp as she ran out of the kitchen. Giovanni ran after her. He was tall and I was sure with his long legs he would close the distance between them in no time. The only advantage Annabelle had was that she was light on her feet. I scrambled up from the floor and took off out the kitchen door and through the house. I spotted Giovanni as he rounded the corner into the foyer.

When I reached the foyer, the front door was wide open and Giovanni was running down the front steps. I sprinted out onto the porch and looked around. Annabelle was sprinting across the lawn, and then she disappeared into the woods. Who knew that she could run that fast?

I ran as fast as my legs would carry me until I finally caught up with Giovanni. I needed something to stop him—something to slow him down so that he couldn't get the book from Annabelle.

I recited the words and pointed my hand toward his back. Giovanni hadn't looked back and didn't even know what hit him when I zapped him with my spell. Power zinged through the air. He collapsed onto the ground and I ran past him. It would take him a while before he could get up and catch up to us. But when I reached the line of trees, I knew that Annabelle had already made it to the other side. At least I hoped she had.

She'd taken off with the book and that had my stomach in knots. She was vulnerable now. What if Giovanni or someone else caught up with her and figured out that she had the book? There was no telling what they would do to her. And she didn't have magic powers to protect herself.

There had to be a way to counteract what Giovanni had done. I had to find a spell that would stop any of his attempts to add spells to the book in the future. Plus, I needed a spell that would delete the words he'd added to the book. We didn't need his poison on the pages. Where had he unleashed this power from? I couldn't believe that he'd been able to achieve something as complicated as that.

CHAPTER NINETEEN

When I turned around, Giovanni was stumbling up from the ground. He glared at me and I shot daggers at him with my eyes. His dirty looks would do nothing to me. But he wouldn't be happy with me for zapping him with that spell.

I marched back over to where he stood. He still seemed a bit dazed from the spell. "I suggest you leave my property now," I demanded as I stood in front of him.

His stare was relentless, but I didn't care. I wasn't about to back down. He stood with his fists clenched by his sides. I was waiting for him to unleash his magic on me, but he turned around and headed back toward his car. I followed him, but I wasn't sure of what he was up to. I knew that this wasn't over. He was probably going to try to find Annabelle.

When he reached his car, he turned to me and said, "I will get that book."

I glared at him, but didn't respond. The coven members were on the veranda, watching me. I was sure they'd watched the whole scene. Now I had to find Annabelle.

He gunned his engine and peeled off down the driveway.

"Is everything okay?" Kelley asked.

"I don't know where Annabelle is and I know he will go looking for her. She's in a great deal of danger as long as she has the book." I rushed my words.

Rebecca tsked. "What a foolish girl."

"She was just trying to help me," I said.

"No matter what she was trying to do, it was foolish." She tossed up her arms and turned around.

The rest of the coven members turned and followed Rebecca back inside the manor. They whispered to each other as they walked, and I knew they were talking about me.

Kelley looked at me with a pitying smile. "I'm sorry. What are you going to do now?"

"I have to find her, but I don't know where she is." The anxiety was evident in my voice.

I ran inside and Kelley followed me. When I rushed into the parlor, I grabbed Annabelle's purse where she'd left it on the small table. I reached inside and found her cell phone. She hadn't taken it with her. I stood there for a moment, unsure of what to do next. Where would Annabelle go? Maybe she would go to her home? Either way, I didn't want to handle Giovanni alone.

"Listen, Kelley, I have to go find Annabelle. I'm going to find Liam and Nicolas so they can help." I grabbed my purse.

"Can I go with you?" Kelley pleaded with her big brown eyes.

I stopped and looked at her. How could I say no?

"I figure you shouldn't try to find them alone. Since you're stressed and all." She gave a half-hearted smile.

I shrugged. "Yeah, I guess that would be okay." The witches watched from the foyer. "Please for the love of all things witchy, don't do any magic while I'm gone."

They nodded and gave little waves in unison. Yeah, I knew there would be spellcasting in the manor while I was gone. They could no more resist the call of magic than I could resist the call of a chocolate bar.

"I figured I can look for my family when I get to town," she said as she climbed into the passenger seat.

"Did you have a lot of family in Enchantment Pointe?" I asked as I navigated out of the drive and down the street.

"I have a few family members. Like I said, my parents died before me." She stared out the window.

"Didn't you want to stay with them on the other side?" I asked.

"Well, it wasn't as if I had a choice. I was brought here, remember?" She looked at me.

"Oh yeah. Again, I am sorry about that," I said, looking at the road again.

We rode in silence for most of the way into Enchantment Pointe. Kelley asked a few questions about current events. It was refreshing to have a spirit who was nice for a change. Kelley stared out the window and absentmindedly played with her bangle bracelets. She turned the radio and found the oldies station, which now meant Eighties music like Duran Duran and Madonna.

When I looked in the rearview mirror, I noticed a car was driving close behind mine. Was it Giovanni again? It didn't look like his car, but I couldn't be sure that he wasn't in a different vehicle now.

I sped up a little but the car sped up too. When I tapped the gas a little more, I noticed a noise coming from the back of the car and the steering wheel began acting strangely. Of all times for me to have car trouble. I had no choice but to pull over. I hoped whoever was following close was just in a hurry. If I pulled over, it would give the driver a chance to go around me.

I steered the car to the side of the road and cut the engine. When I stepped out, Kelley jumped out too and followed me to the back of the car. The big problem was that the strange white car had also stopped and pulled up behind my car. My heart rate increased as the gray-haired man climbed out from behind the wheel and walked toward us.

"Do you know that man?" Kelley asked.

I shook my head. "No, I've never seen him."

The man approached the car. I hoped he wasn't a killer.

"I was trying to get close enough to tell you that there was a problem with your back wheel. I hope I didn't scare you, but you sped up when I got close."

I looked down at the back of my car. Sure enough, the tire was almost flat. I groaned. What would I do now?

"Thank you so much," I said with a smile.

"Do you need help?" he asked.

I didn't want to tell him that I was just going to fix the flat with a little magic.

"No, I'll be fine. Thank you." I said.

He nodded. "Take care," he said as he walked back to his car.

I watched as he drove off. He'd seemed honest and I knew that I was just being paranoid. It was probably a good thing he'd come along to help when he did, although I was lucky that I had magic to help me. I was sure someone had caused the flat tire—my guess was Giovanni. The stranger had probably caused Giovanni to abandon his attempt to confront me on this isolated road.

"I'll just fix it with a little magic, it'll be a lot faster than if we'd let him help." I stepped closer to the car and pushed the sleeves of my sweater up, as if I was about to get dirty.

Kelley nodded. "Let me know if I can help."

I had to admit I'd never changed a tire. Now that I thought about it, fixing a flat was probably a skill I should have learned.

I recited the words for a spell as Kelley stood beside me. This time there was no wind, no lights, no magic-charged air. When I looked down at the flat, it did nothing. I frowned.

"That's not what was supposed to happen," I said.

Now that the spell hadn't worked, Kelley and I would have to figure out how to fix it on our own.

"Maybe I can help," she said. "Although my witchcraft is probably a little rusty. I haven't used it in a while."

I guessed it was worth a shot. Kelley pointed her hands toward the tire, but before she had a chance to recite any words or do any magic, the tire instantly was fixed.

I looked at her. "Did you do something?"

She shook her head. "No, I hadn't even started my magic."

As we headed back to the car, I glanced over at Kelley. I noticed the symbol sewn onto the bottom of her shirt right away. Why hadn't I noticed it earlier? It was just like the symbol on the witches' clothing.

"What is that symbol on your shirt?" I asked as I started the car.

She glanced down. "Oh, that's a witch's symbol. Just for good luck. I don't remember how I heard about it, but I think it helps with spells."

I stared at her for a moment. "That's odd. The coven members have that symbol."

She chuckled. "Well, it isn't helping with their magic, huh?"

I smiled. "No, I suppose it isn't."

CHAPTER TWENTY

Annabelle lived in a beige-colored brick ranch in a small subdivision of newer homes. I drove up to Annabelle's home and parked the car in the driveway. After rushing from behind the wheel, I hurried up to the door and pounded on it. When she didn't answer, I went around to all the windows and peeked in. Nothing seemed out of place. Everything was neat, just as Annabelle always left it. Sunlight streamed through the opposite window and lit up the rooms. Her living room was on the left and the dining room on the right with the kitchen behind it.

Going back to the door, I found the key that she'd given me in my purse and opened the door.

"Annabelle, are you here?" I called out.

I went from room to room, but she was nowhere in sight. There was a glass in the sink, but other than that the kitchen was spotless. The table had been cleaned off. I knew Annabelle's routine was to clean up every morning. It looked as if she hadn't been home since she'd left.

"Looks like she's not here," Kelley said.

"No, and I don't think she's been here either. I'm not sure where to look next, but maybe she went to find the guys too. We should head over there now," I said.

Kelley and I climbed back into the car and made our way over to the Bubbling Cauldron. Nicolas' car was parked on the street in front of the bar.

"Wow. This place was a grocery store when I was alive," Kelley said as she walked beside me.

"Yes, I guess a few things have changed, huh?" I asked.

"Yeah, but they've made good improvements. They used to have a Pac Man game in there that I played every day after classes," Kelley said.

"They don't really have those anymore. Although I'm sure there are some around. You can play it on your cell phone now." I held up my phone.

"Where's the bag for your phone?" she asked.

I snorted. "No bag for the cell phone needed either."

Her hair still had an amazing amount of Aqua Net and her bangs reached skyward at a height I'd previously thought gravity would never allow, so I wasn't surprised that she still wondered about all things Eighties.

I dialed Nicolas and Liam's numbers, but neither answered my calls. It went straight to voicemail. Of course that upped my anxiety level even more.

When we reached the door, Nicolas and Liam were coming out of the bar.

"Why didn't you guys answer your phones?" I asked exasperated.

"It's strange, but they wouldn't work," Nicolas said, holding up his phone. "If I didn't know better, I'd think someone had placed a spell on them so that they won't work."

"What's going on?" Liam asked with a scowl on his face.

"Annabelle is gone with the Book of Mystics," I said.

"What? What the hell happened?" Liam asked.

Nicolas stepped closer to me and touched my arm. "Tell me what happened."

"Giovanni showed up and the coven ladies thought it would be a good idea to see if he could add a spell to the book," I said. Liam shook his head and Nicolas frowned. "They thought it would solve the problem once and for all if he couldn't add a spell."

"Let me guess, he added a spell," Liam said.

I frowned and shook my head. "Yes, that's when I grabbed the book. He lunged for it, and Annabelle snatched it and took off into the woods."

"What did Giovanni do?" Nicolas asked.

"He went after her, but I zapped him. He got mad and took off," I said.

"So you tried to call Annabelle, I guess?" Liam asked.

I nodded. "She left her purse and phone at the manor. I went by her house, but she's not there."

Nicolas and Liam exchanged a look.

"What do we do now?" Kelley asked.

Just then my cell phone rang. "Maybe that's her," I said as I answered.

"I have the spellbook," my mother said.

CHAPTER TWENTY-ONE

"How did you get the book? Where is Annabelle?" I asked in a panic.

"She left the book with me. She's not here. I can't believe you let it get out of your sight. And it's too late because the coven already knows," my mother said.

"I don't care if they know, Mother," I said angrily.

"Well, don't snap at me because you lost the book," she said.

"I'll be there in two minutes," I said. We were close enough to walk to my mother's shop.

"What happened?" Nicolas asked.

"The book is at my mother's, but apparently Annabelle isn't there," I said.

As we were walking toward my mother's shop, my phone rang again. I exchanged a look with Nicolas. When I answered, I was relieved to hear Annabelle's voice. "Where are you?" I asked.

"Did you get the book back?" she asked as she tried to catch her breath.

"I'm on my way to get the book, but it sounds like you've been running. Is everything okay? Where are you?"

"I can't talk right now, but I have something important to tell you. I'll meet you at…"

The phone went dead.

"Hello? Hello? Annabelle?" I said.

There was no answer, so I immediately dialed her number again, but it went straight to her voicemail.

"What is going on with the cell phones today?" I said as I hung up the phone.

"What did Annabelle say?" Liam asked.

"She said she wanted to meet me, but the phone went dead."

Finally my mother's shop came into view. We weaved around traffic as we crossed the street and walked into the store. When we rushed in the door my mother was standing there with her hands on her hips.

"Well, what kind of mess have you gotten into now?" She looked at us, then focused her attention on Kelley's hair. "Oh, dear. Is it a costume party?"

Kelley frowned.

"Mother, this is Kelley. She's the witch I accidentally brought back from the Eighties," I said.

"Oh, for goodness' sake, when will this end," my mother said.

I glared at her. "I don't have time to argue with you right now. Where is the book?"

She reached under the counter and handed it to me. "It's a good thing you have your mother to look out for you."

I felt heat rush to my cheeks. I looked like a complete idiot because I'd let the book get away. "Where did Annabelle go when she left the book?" I asked, taking the book from her hands.

"She left with Misty Middleton and some man who said he was a bartender at the Bubbling Cauldron."

That didn't sound right. What was she doing with them? Annabelle had never cared much for Misty. "Did she say why she left?" I asked with a frown.

My mother shook her head. "No, they were secretive, which I found a little odd."

"We should find out what's going on," Nicolas said.

"Thank you, Mom, for taking care of the book. Now we have to find Annabelle."

She looked at all of us and shook her head. "Is there anything I can do?"

"Yes, call me if she shows up here again," I said.

"Well, I tried to call you, but the phone wasn't working. Maybe you should think about getting a new service provider," she said with a frown.

"I'll think about that," I said.

Now that I had the book back, I had to find Annabelle to make sure she was okay. With our cell phones not working, it would be kind of hard to call Misty.

"We'll have to go to Misty's home," I said.

"Let's go," Liam said, holding the door open for Kelley and me.

"Thank you, Mrs. LaVeau," Nicolas said, waving to my mother.

My mother blushed and wiggled her hand in a flirty wave.

"I hope I remember which house is Misty's," I said as we rushed back to my car.

We loaded into the car with Nicolas and Liam in the back seat and headed toward the other side of town. It would be hard not to speed because I couldn't get there fast enough. Something wasn't right and I had to figure it out before it was too late.

As I drove down the main street, I glanced over at the sidewalk. "Hey, there's Annabelle."

I whipped the car over in front of several cars, causing angry honks. I steered over to the side of the road and tapped the horn. Annabelle jumped and clutched her chest. A look of relief fell over her face when she saw us. I shoved the car into park and cut the engine. We all jumped out and rushed over to her.

"What is going on? Are you okay? I was worried about you," I said.

"Sorry about that, but my cell phone isn't working," Annabelle said.

"Yeah, it seems like no one's phone is working lately. Where have you been?" I asked.

"I was with Misty Middleton and that guy from the bar who said he was her friend." Annabelle's neatly plucked eyebrows furrowed.

"I take it from your expression that you don't think he's really a friend," I said.

Annabelle frowned and shook her head. "No, I don't think he is. I overheard him talking and he was talking with that Giovanni."

"Damn it," Liam said.

"I knew it. I knew we couldn't trust this guy," I said.

"What else did he say?" Nicolas asked.

"He was supposed to meet Giovanni, but he told him that he didn't have the book yet. I guess that made Giovanni mad because I think they were arguing on the phone," Annabelle said.

"It's funny that their phones work," Kelley pointed out.

She was right. I'd have to find out which service they used.

"Why were you with Misty?" I asked.

"She said that she had something for you and it was a surprise. In hindsight, maybe I shouldn't have been so gullible," Annabelle said.

"What was it?" I asked. I didn't care if it was supposed to be a surprise, something told me this wouldn't be a gift that I would want.

"I don't know, I never saw it. As soon as I overheard the conversation, I took off. They're probably looking for me now," Annabelle said.

I narrowed my eyes. This made me furious. I didn't know what tricks they were up to, but I had to find out. "First, I need to take the book back and make sure it's in a secure location, then we need to find Misty Middleton," I said.

"Why don't you let us find Misty and Kevin and you go back to the manor with the book?" Nicolas asked.

"That sounds like a good idea," I said.

We drove Nicolas and Liam back to his car and then we headed back to the manor.

"I'll try to call you. If the phone will work," Nicolas said as he climbed out of the car.

We exchanged a look. Nicolas' eyes held strength, but underneath there was an uneasy worry. As much as he tried, he couldn't hide it from me.

I watched for a moment as the men walked away. Liam turned around and gave me a reassuring nod. How had he known that was just what I'd needed at the moment?

"I can't believe you took off with the book like that," I said to Annabelle as we steered away from the curb.

"Sorry about that," Annabelle said with a sigh. "I didn't know what else to do and the impulse hit me, so I ran with it. Literally." She snorted.

"No, I'm glad you did because I don't know what would have happened if you hadn't taken the book," I said.

She smiled. "Thanks. This paranormal stuff is crazy."

She could say that again.

We pulled up to the manor and hopped out. This time I had a tight hold on the book in case Giovanni showed up again.

CHAPTER TWENTY-TWO

A strange vibe overwhelmed me. I'd experienced the oddness before, but this was different now. How it was different I didn't know. Something was off and it felt like it was coming from inside the house. When I experienced this in the past it had always come from black magic or a demon. My sense of awareness kept me on edge and alert.

A sickening feeling washed over me just thinking about what I'd been through in the past couple weeks. Was this what it was going to be like for the rest of the time I was the leader? How long would I be the leader? It looked as if my days were numbered.

We parked in front of the manor and made our way inside. Once I stepped inside, the sensation grew stronger. It was thick in the air.

"Do you feel that?" I asked.

Kelley shook her head. "I don't sense anything odd if that's what you mean."

"Maybe I'm being overly sensitive," I said.

When I stepped into the parlor, I let out a little gasp. "What the hell happened?"

The coven members froze. Rebecca had a sofa leg in her hand and Barbara had a coffee table leg in her hand.

The chairs were broken too. The whole room was in shambles.

"What the hell happened in here?" I asked.

Everyone stood around speechless. Finally, Rebecca said, "We were performing a spell and I guess it got a little out of hand."

"A little? What kind of spell were you trying?" I asked.

"We just wanted to make things easier for you," Sarah said.

I quirked a brow. "What is that supposed to mean?"

"Meaning we were trying to do housework for you," Rebecca said.

No wonder I'd felt a strange vibe when we'd pulled up to the manor. "What else have you done?" My stomach turned.

They exchanged a look and I knew the damage wasn't over.

"Well, we tried to do your laundry for you," Kimberley said.

My face was probably drained of color. "What happened to my clothes?" I asked.

They looked down at the floor, but wouldn't answer me. I ran toward the laundry room, which was next to the kitchen. When I went into the room, I saw my clothing all over the place. I picked up a shirt and it had holes on the front and back. Another shirt was now pink instead of white.

"We're sorry about that," Rebecca said from over my shoulder.

"Why are you performing spells?"

"We're witches. What do you expect us to do?" Kimberly said.

"I expect you not to destroy my house and my belongings. You're not very good witches."

"Well, aren't you the kettle calling the cauldron black," Rebecca said.

I'd have to tackle that problem later. I didn't have time to deal with this. I just had to pray that they wouldn't burn the manor down while I was gone. I had to find out what the spell was that Giovanni added and what it meant, plus find Misty.

When I reached the parlor again, I discovered Liam and Nicolas were picking up the mess. "You're back. Did you find Misty?" I asked.

Nicolas ran his hand through his hair. "No, we couldn't find her."

"I need your help with finding out what the spell that Giovanni added means and then we'll find Misty too."

"What can we do?" Liam asked as he turned one of the chairs upright again.

"I guess we need to find Giovanni or the very least find out who he is. Why is he so mysterious? Where did he come from? Why did he pop up all of a sudden? Why not sooner?"

"You're just full of questions," Liam said with a smile.

"If I find Misty Middleton maybe she can provide answers. She needs to tell me why she was with the bartender. I know he is connected to Giovanni now," I said.

I pulled out my cell phone and dialed Misty's number, but it still went straight to her voicemail.

The witches stepped back into the room with innocent looks on their faces.

"I think you all have done enough magic for the day, don't you think?" I asked.

"The night is young and we thought we'd go back to that bar you showed us," Barbara said.

Nicolas looked at me. "You took them to a bar?"

"Not on purpose. They kind of tagged along when I went to talk with Misty Middleton," I said.

"Ladies, I really don't think it's a good idea that you all go there," Liam said.

Barbara placed her hands on her hips. "You don't want us to have fun?"

"You can't tell us what to do," Rebecca said with a scowl.

The women marched toward the door. When Nicolas opened the door, Jon was standing there. I knew he'd said he really didn't know Kevin, but I couldn't help my suspicion.

"I came to pick up Annabelle," he said.

"Don't you want to go to the bar with us?" I asked.

Annabelle shook her head. "It's tempting, but I think I'll pass. Call me soon, okay?"

I nodded. "I'll call you soon."

An uneasy feeling engulfed me as I watched Annabelle leave with Jon. There was nothing I could do though. There was no proof that he had anything to do with Kevin or all of this craziness.

"Looks like we're going to the bar," I said.

"It looks that way," Nicolas said.

I groaned. This would not end well. I knew the women would get in trouble. The only question was how much.

"What do you say, Liam, are you ready for the Bubbling Cauldron?" I asked.

The witches batted their eyelashes at him and flashed huge smiles. If he knew what was good for him he'd ignore their flirting. It would lead to nothing but problems.

"I think I'll just wait here, if that's okay? In case Misty, Giovanni or Kevin comes back."

I nodded. "That'll be good. Thanks."

I knew it was probably wise that he stay behind, but I wished he'd come along with us.

I stopped the women as we approached the door. "Ladies, there is a no-magic policy at the bar. Do you understand?" I asked.

They nodded. "Of course. Why would we cast a spell there?" Kimberly said.

"Why would you cast a spell in my kitchen?" I asked drily.

When I stepped out onto the porch, a ghost of a breeze floated past. Moss hung on tree limbs like sheets of lace, swaying with the wind. The motion lulled the area into a false calm. I wasn't fooled by this deceptive tranquility.

As I moved down the steps, I said, "Oh, will you look at that. I forgot you all can't fit in my car, not with Nicolas, too. I guess we'll just have to cancel this trip."

The women batted their eyelashes at Nicolas. "Barbara and I can ride with Nicolas. He has a car," Rebecca said with a smile.

There was no way I could do that to Nicolas. "I don't think that would be a good idea," I said.

"I'll make sure they don't do anything on the ride there," Nicolas said. "Once we get there I can't guarantee that I'll be able to keep an eye on them though."

"That's what I'm afraid of." I sighed as the women all stared at me. "Fine, but we can't stay long. I have to rest. I honestly don't know where you all get your energy from," I said as I climbed behind the wheel.

I glanced in my rearview mirror and saw Rebecca sitting in the front seat of Nicolas' car. She looked absolutely giddy. As soon as I turned out onto the highway, Kimberly turned on the radio. I reached over and turned down the volume.

"Do they have more snacks other than pretzels at this bar?" Kimberly asked.

As soon as we walked through the door of the Bubbling Cauldron, the witches took off for the dance floor. I soon lost sight of them in the crowd. I knew they would want to check out the cauldron again, so I forced my way through the swaying bodies toward the cauldron.

When I reached the giant black cauldron, the witches weren't there. People circled around the bubbles, but the witches had all but vanished.

A guy wearing a red plaid shirt and skintight jeans pushed his body against me. "Do you want to dance, baby?"

I pushed his chest with my hand and hurried around him. Nicolas had been looking on the other side for the witches, but he caught up with me. "Do you see them?"

I shook my head. "They're not here."

A blonde woman watched me as she stood by the edge of the dance floor. I stepped over to her and asked, "Have you seen a group of witches wearing large witch hats?"

She took a sip of her drink and spoke over the noise, "Yeah, I thought I saw them leave with another young woman."

Nicolas grabbed my hand. "Let's get out of here. It's too crowded."

"We can't leave the witches," I said.

"The place will close soon. We'll have no choice but leave."

I scanned the crowd again. "Yeah, I guess you're right. Do you really think they left with someone?"

"Probably not. I'll bet they stepped outside. They're probably headed back to the manor."

"But how will they get there?" I asked.

Knowing the witches, they probably caught a ride," Nicolas said.

"That's what I'm afraid of."

I couldn't believe we'd lost the witches at the bar. I hadn't wanted to leave the witches there, but I had no choice. I left my number with the bartender with instructions to call me if the witches showed up again.

"Don't worry. They'll find their way back." Nicolas's mouth curled into a reassuring smile.

***

Liam was asleep on the sofa when we returned. He looked so peaceful and handsome. A dark tendril of hair rested on his forehead and I resisted the urge to gently push it back. Instead I reached down and gently touched his arm. He opened his eyes and for a moment we stared at each other in silence.

When he realized others were around, he jumped up. "What happened?"

"It's okay. We're back from the bar. We lost the witches," I said.

"What? How did that happen?" he asked.

I shook my head. "I guess they blended in with the crowd."

We sat around the parlor in silence. Everyone was lost in their own thoughts. Liam tapped his fingers against the chair. Nicolas leaned back and stared blankly at the wall. I tried to calm by nerves with even steady breaths.

"I just remembered something," Kelley said as she stood up from the one of the few remaining chairs in the room that hadn't been broken. "I saw something at the plantation that I think was Giovanni's."

I froze. "What do you mean something that you thought was his? What was it and what makes you think it was his?" Why hadn't she mentioned this earlier? It was kind of an important detail to leave out considering she knew that I'd been looking for him.

"It looked like a pouch with a symbol on the front. I went outside and picked it up. The odd thing is, it looks like the one I have on my shirt and the witches have on their skirts."

This revelation sent my head spinning. I didn't know what to think. "What did you do with it?" I asked.

She pulled the pouch from her pocket and dangled it through the air. "I put it in my pocket."

I was sure my mouth hung open. "But how do you know it was his?" I asked as I stepped closer and took the pouch from her outstretched hand.

"I saw someone who looked like Giovanni drop it." She shrugged. "So I guess I can't say for sure that it was him. But we should definitely go to the plantation and look for him."

That was more than enough for me. This was becoming more complicated by the second. "I have to find Giovanni St. Clair," I said.

CHAPTER TWENTY-THREE

The bayou surrounded the plantation. Darkness was moving in and clouds quickly covered the sky, blocking out the moon and stars. Moss-draped oak trees lined the long driveway, stretching out in front of the plantation.

Two large porches wrapped around the bottom and top floors of the plantation with massive columns on the front façade. The only light came from the front parlor. It cast an eerie glow that let me know that people were waiting in that room for us. I wasn't sure what to expect—but I knew I had to be ready for anything.

We made our way up the massive steps, but before approaching the front door, it swung open.

"Please come in." A middle-aged woman with chestnut hair gestured for us to enter as she stepped out of the way.

Once inside, to my left was the parlor and on the right was the library. Books lined the shelves and wingback chairs sat in front of the fireplace. But no one was waiting for us in that room, everyone had gathered in the parlor.

As I stepped into the parlor, I looked around at the expectant faces. Fine furnishings and high ceilings highlighted the opulence of the room. A massive crystal chandelier hung in the middle of the room.

New Orleans coven members were sitting around the parlor on the left when we entered. There were many faces that I'd never seen before. They were the coven members who'd recently joined the coven again. A couple men sat next to the window and two more stood by the fireplace. Several women sat on the sofa.

Kelley had suggested that I bring the Book of Mystics with me to fight Giovanni if we found him, but I hadn't wanted to take it from its safe place.

"We came to help," a woman said as she pushed to her feet.

I looked around the room at all the people watching me. "Why do you want to help?" I asked.

"We want you to be the leader. We want Liam to be the New Orleans Coven leader. All of that will change if someone else comes into power. Liam has been talking about you nonstop. He has so many wonderful things to say about you. When you got rid of the bad coven members and made Liam the leader, we were able to join the coven again," she said.

I glanced over at Liam. He was looking out the window and didn't meet my gaze. When I glanced at Nicolas he had a worried look on his face. I couldn't believe that Liam had talked about me. I wondered what exactly he'd said.

"I don't know what to say," I said, running my hand through my hair and releasing a deep breath.

"Just tell us what you need us to do," she said.

"Well, I'm not sure exactly. We need to find Giovanni."

A woman appeared from the foyer. She had long blonde hair that swept away from her face. She wore bright red lipstick that looked gorgeous on her full lips. Her black dress hit every curve in just the right place.

"I saw Giovanni get in the car with Misty and another man," she said, looking right at me.

"When did this happen?" I asked.

"It was about an hour ago," she said.

"What were they doing here? Did they come inside the plantation?" I asked.

She shrugged as she moved across the room. She sat down on the arm of the sofa and crossed her legs. "I have no idea why they were here and, no, they didn't come inside. I watched from the window."

Did the coven members stay here often when Liam wasn't here? Had there been a meeting?

"Is there anything else you aren't telling us?" I asked, crossing my arms in front of my chest.

She stared for a minute, then said, "I overheard that they were headed to that vampire bar. The popular one."

"Was it called the Graveyard?" Liam asked.

She nodded. "Yeah, that's the one."

"Let's go to the Graveyard," I said, making my way to the door.

We hurried outside and climbed into the car. "I'll drive if you want me to," Liam offered.

Good idea considering I wasn't sure exactly how to get to the bar. I'd only been there a couple of times.

"If they were going to the vampire bar then that means at least one of them had to be a vampire, right? Why else would they go there?" I asked.

"They'd probably go to a witches' bar instead," Kelley said.

I sat in the backseat with Nicolas and Kelley sat up front with Liam. When I looked up, Liam was looking at me through the rear-view mirror. I could have sworn he was looking at my lips. Was he thinking about the kiss that we'd shared? Nicolas squeezed my hand, bringing me away from the exchange with Liam. I don't think he'd noticed that Liam was watching me, but I couldn't be sure.

We finally pulled up to the bar and found a parking spot. The place was busy and people walked in all directions, coming and going from the bar and surrounding businesses. Music spilled out from the building, invading the night air. After making our way past the large bouncer, we stepped into the bar and it was crammed with people. How would we ever find Misty? Tables surrounded the edges of the space with the dance floor in the middle. Pulsating lights covered the area in an alternating blue, red and yellow glow. Loud conversations, even louder music, and clinking of glasses hurt my ears.

"I don't think we'll be able to find them," I said, looking around the room.

"How about Kelley and I look on this side and you and Nicolas can look on the other side," Liam said.

I nodded. "Sounds like a good idea."

Nicolas grabbed my hand and we took off across the crowded bar. We weaved through the crowd, looking at the faces standing and sitting around the room. In the corner of the room, I spotted them. Misty, Giovanni and Kevin were sitting at a table, talking and drinking. Giovanni paused as if he sensed me, but so far they hadn't noticed us.

I nudged Nicolas and pointed them out. "There they are."

We headed across the room and I didn't let them out of my sight. I didn't want them to get away from us. My stomach did a flip. I wondered what kind of confrontation this was going to be. Would Giovanni start a fight right there in the middle of the bar? Before we could make it through the crowd, the men stood and walked away, in the opposite direction.

"They're leaving." I pointed.

Misty was still sitting at the table with her back facing us. As far as I could tell she still didn't know we were there. When we reached the table, I tapped her on the shoulder. When Misty spun around, she jumped and knocked over her drink.

"Hallie!" She chuckled nervously and clutched her chest. "What are you doing here?"

"Maybe the better question is what are you doing here?" I said.

She picked up her glass and tried to soak up the spilled liquid with her cocktail napkin. She was avoiding my gaze.

"Why did you come to this bar with them? Why are you in a vampire bar?" I asked.

Nicolas and I stood in front of her, staring down, waiting for an answer. She shook her head as if she didn't want to answer.

"You know I won't let you get by without giving me an answer and don't even think about lying to me," I said.

"Okay," she said, holding her hands up. "Giovanni said he was going to be the new leader of the Underworld and that I should help him. He said that he would give me a special position in the Underworld. We came to meet a vampire Giovanni knows, but he never showed up."

I glared at her. "I should have known."

"I'm sorry, Hallie. But I really wanted the new job," she said.

"You think he was going to really give you some great position with the Underworld? The man is a liar."

She shrugged as if to say she wasn't so sure he was lying.

"Where did they go?" I demanded.

"They were headed to another bar, but I don't know which one," she said.

I glared at her. "I swear if you are lying to me, you will be sorry."

"I swear, Hallie, I don't know which bar they were going to. I know it was a witches' bar here in New Orleans," she said.

I studied her face to see if she was really lying to me. I wasn't sure if I was a good judge of character, but it seemed as if she was being honest for a change.

"We have to find out where Giovanni went," Nicolas said. "Misty, you're coming with us."

She stood without protest and we followed as she walked through the crowd. I wasn't about to let her get out of my sight now. I figured she'd take off running the first chance she got. I'd give her one more chance to tell me what she knew.

"Misty, now that I'm the leader I don't think you should keep anything from me. If you know where they went now is the time to be completely honest," I said.

She looked over at me with apprehension in her eyes. Finally, she said, "They went to Spells and Spirits."

"Thank you." I knew she hadn't wanted to give me the name, but now wasn't the time for her games.

We made our way through the crowd and finally spotted Kelley and Liam. They were at the front of the bar, talking with a group of men. Liam was gesturing around the bar. It didn't look as if this was a friendly confrontation. Before we approached the men turned around and walked out the door.

When I approached Liam I asked, "What was that all about?"

Liam shrugged. "They were just drunk, that's all. They told us to get out of the bar."

Kelley attempted a smile, but I felt like they were keeping something from me, as if something was wrong. I didn't have time to debate it now though. Liam looked at Misty and she had to know he wasn't happy with her either.

"I see you found Misty," Liam said.

I glanced over at her. "She was with Giovanni and Kevin, but before we could get there they took off. She claims they were headed to some bar named Spells and Spirits. I have no idea where that is."

"I know where it is. Let's go." Liam headed toward the door and we followed. Did he know where every bar was? I made Misty walk in front of us.

As we walked outside into the warm fall air, Misty glanced back at me. "Who is the girl with Liam and what's with her clothes?" Misty asked.

There was no way I wanted to tell her that I'd brought Misty back from the 1980s. "I think she's a friend of Liam's," I said as I quickened my steps.

"You *think?*" Misty frowned as she matched my pace.

"Okay, yes, she is," I said, not looking over at Misty.

"She looks very familiar," Misty said. "I know her from somewhere. Where's she from?"

I glanced over at her. There was no way she could know her, right? "I'm not sure where she's from," I said quickly.

Misty quirked an eyebrow. "I'm shocked that you haven't asked a million questions about her. Are they dating?"

My stomach did a flip at the mention. "Um, no, I don't think they are, but I don't know."

"She'd be pretty if only she wasn't wearing that clothing. Does she have a thing for Eighties? Madonna?" she asked.

"Yeah, I think that's it," I said quickly.

"Well, I don't know where I know her from, but it'll come to me eventually. I never forget a face," she said.

When we finally reached the car I realized it was going to be a tight fit. Liam and Kelley sat in the front again. I was stuck in the backseat between Nicolas and Misty. Her strong floral perfume was already giving me a headache. A little went a long way. We were stuffed into the car so tightly that I wondered if we'd ever get out.

Misty leaned forward in the seat. Oh no, she was going to start asking Kelley questions. Why couldn't she just let it go? Didn't she have enough to worry about? Like me possibly stripping her of her coven leader status?

"Excuse me." She tapped Kelley on the shoulder. Kelley looked back with a confused stare. "Don't I know you from somewhere?" Misty asked.

Couldn't Liam turn up the music or something?

"Probably not. I just got here," Kelley said. Oh, thank goodness she didn't tell on me.

"Where are you from?" Misty pushed for more details.

"I'm from Enchantment Pointe," Kelley said.

Misty frowned. "Then why don't I know you?"

"That's because I just came back after a very long time away," Kelley said.

Misty seemed to ponder this for a moment. Finally, she leaned back in her seat. I hoped that she'd finally let it go. But I knew by the look on her face that she'd probably approach the topic again.

CHAPTER TWENTY-FOUR

Liam navigated the French Quarter streets and we rode in silence. It was actually quite awkward. The bar wasn't far, and I was thankful when we finally arrived so I could get out of the cramped backseat.

Spells and Spirits was in an old building, but it had lots of neon lights with potion bottles and other gimmicky symbols splashed across the front. We finally made our way through the crowd on the sidewalk and got inside the club.

The music was pumping. Bodies were packed into the place and the pace at which people were moving across the space was incredibly slow.

"There is no way we'll ever find them in here."

"You need to try a spell," Nicolas said.

I quirked a brow. "What? What kind of spell? What if something goes wrong?"

"What could go wrong?" He bit his lip. "Oh well, I'm sure things will be fine. It will be better if you do the spell because you are the one looking for Giovanni the most."

I began reciting the spell. It was specifically stated on the outside sign that no spells were allowed—just like every witch bar. But I was the leader and this was an emergency—surely there would be no problem with that.

Suddenly the crowd thinned out and the men came into view. The club seemed to come to a halt. Giovanni and Kevin spotted me. Giovanni glared and raised his arm up. He pointed at me and I braced for the spell that I knew was about to hit me. Multi-colored lights zinged across the room. It was like a light show. Screams and gasps rang out across the room.

I fell backward and landed on my butt. He'd definitely knocked the wind out of me. The men must have cast a spell on everyone, because people seemed to be frozen to the spot. I stumbled up and pointed at them, reciting the words. I pulled energy from Liam and Nicolas. Of course Misty and Kelley didn't offer to allow me to use their energy.

Giovanni and Kevin took off across the room and disappeared down a dark, narrow hallway. Liam, Nicolas and I took off running in that direction. When we reached the hallway we spotted a door. We opened it and stepped out into the alley, but the men were nowhere in sight. Nicolas checked behind the Dumpsters, but didn't find the men. When I caught a whiff of the nearby trash, I regretted inhaling. And the last thing I wanted to see was a rat.

"They got away again," I said, letting out a deep breath.

"Are you okay?" Nicolas asked as he grabbed my arm.

"Yeah, I'm okay." I nodded.

"Let's get back inside and ask if anyone knows where they were headed," Liam said.

When we returned inside the main area of the club, the music had stopped and people were standing around talking. All eyes were on us when we entered. They stopped talking and stared at me. The frowns on their faces took me off guard.

A man stomped over to us. "What the hell is going on here? Didn't you read the sign?" he asked with venom in his voice.

"My name is Hallie LaVeau. I'm the new leader of the Underworld. I'm sorry about the magic, but we have a bit of a problem with those men. Do you know them or where they might have gone?" I gestured over my shoulder.

The man didn't look impressed that I was the leader. "I know who you are. He told me all about you. You should give him the book," he said.

I couldn't believe what I was hearing. People had gathered around now and I was beginning to think that we should get out of there soon. They seemed to be forming a mob and it looked like they were ready to knock me out.

"All these people aren't happy with you either and they want you out as leader," he said. They all glared at me.

This definitely wasn't going as planned. It looked like it was time for us to get out of there. "If you'll excuse me, we'll be leaving now," I said.

I couldn't believe that Giovanni had already told people about me. Who else had he already told about the situation? Soon he'd have the whole Underworld against me. I had to get to the bottom of this soon. There was no telling what would happen if I didn't.

People gathered around, circling us. "I think it's time we get out of here, Hallie," Liam said.

I nodded. "Yeah, that's a good idea."

Everyone watched us as we moved across the space. Misty and Kelley were still waiting by the front door. When I looked back, everyone had stopped moving and seemed to be frozen in time. This was not a good sign.

"What is going on?" Kelley asked.

"I don't know, but Giovanni told these people that I'm the enemy."

"I can see that," she said as she looked around the room.

The room was still standing still. I had to stop the spell that Giovanni had cast. I reached my arms out and recited the words. Lights and wind flashed and flew across the space. But it did nothing but make everyone collapse onto the floor. That definitely wasn't the right spell.

Kelley stepped forward. "I've seen a spell like this before. Can I help?"

I shrugged. Where had she seen this spell before? Why did her magic work and not mine?

She whipped her arms around and the wind and lights seemed to do the right thing this time. Everyone climbed up from the floor. They seemed dazed at first, but soon their confusion turned to confrontation and they were glaring at us. We had recreated a hostile environment. Nicolas grabbed my arm.

"I think we've made a few people mad," Liam said coyly.

I needed for Misty to tell me everything that had happened. "If you don't tell me everything, I will have to take away your position as the leader of the Enchantment Pointe Coven," I said.

Her mouth dropped open. "You can't do that."

I stared at her.

"Well, I guess you can, but I don't know anything. All he wanted was the book and I told him I wasn't sure if I could get it," she said.

I knew what she was thinking. She thought that I didn't have the right to fire her. She felt that Giovanni was the leader and should make that choice. But as of right now I was still the leader, and it was still my job to make sure the coven leaders did the right thing.

Maybe the men had decided to go back to the vampire bar, but I didn't want to play a game of cat-and-mouse all night. It was time to give up for the evening. Maybe I would think of a new plan in the morning. I certainly hoped so because I was currently all out of ideas. I thought

everyone else was out of ideas too. If they weren't, they
sure weren't telling me about them.

CHAPTER TWENTY-FIVE

When we arrived at the manor that night, the coven members had already returned. I had no idea how they had got there because they were tight-lipped about events. Heck, they could have flown back on brooms for all I knew.

A noise sounded in the middle of the night. The old manor made lots of creaks and groans, but I'd learned the difference. This was more than an old place settling. Something... or someone was down there.

Nicolas and I wasted little time jumping from bed. We headed downstairs to check it out. My eyes finally adjusted to the darkness as I descended the grand staircase. Nicolas led the way and I was right behind him, holding his bare arm. There was no sound now other than my heavy breathing.

With each step forward my anxiety grew. What if someone had broken into the house? What if another evil spirit had found its way to LaVeau Manor. There were too many what-ifs for my mind to even comprehend.

Noise sounded again and I knew it came from outside. When we reached the front door, Nicolas peeked out the front door.

"It's Giovanni," he said, opening the door and running out after him.

I took off after Nicolas. When my eyes finally adjusted to the darkness, I spotted Giovanni running into the woods that surrounded LaVeau Manor. Oak and pine trees filled the area. Each time I stepped under the canopy of trees, it was like being carried away to another world.

Nicolas and I headed into the woods to see if we could find Giovanni. If that had really been him then we were determined to confront him. He had no reason to be at the manor. All he wanted to do was cause trouble.

After we found him and told him to get lost, then I had to try to find a spell that would banish him from returning forever. I didn't care if he did claim the book was his—until I knew for sure, he needed to stay away.

We finally reached the line of trees and stepped into the darkened area under the shade of the tall trees. The air was cooler and silence encircled us. The scent of earth and pine filled the air. This was where Nicolas had first traced the delicate skin of my neck with his fangs. My heart sped up just thinking about it—the thought of something so intimate was a little thrilling and scary at the same time. I wasn't sure how I felt about it, but it was something I would have to discuss with him soon. Giovanni was nowhere in sight.

"Are you sure you saw him?" Nicolas asked.

I nodded. "I'm positive. I don't think he would have had time to get to the other side yet."

We walked deeper into the woods, but there was still no sign of Giovanni. This was getting old quickly. He'd probably pulled off a spell that was concealing himself from view. I wouldn't lie, it made me angry that he was better at magic than me. Maybe he should be the leader. I mean, after all, I had no clue what I was doing.

The air changed around us. It was like breathing through a thick cloud, energized with emotion. My senses were on full alert. I knew that Nicolas felt my anxiety.

"Do you feel that?" Nicolas asked.

I nodded. "Yes, I think he's playing games with us."

Nicolas nodded and looked around. "Come on, let's keep going."

Nicolas and I headed out across the area. I knew once we made it to the other side that we'd come upon my neighbor's home. I hoped that Giovanni didn't pay her a visit. She was a nice lady and she'd even kept some of my great-aunt Maddy's things and given them to me.

The air continued to change around us and I grew more anxious by the minute. I expected Giovanni to pop out at any moment. We'd almost reached the edge of the woods when we stepped forward and smashed into something—something unseen by the naked eye. It was as if we'd stepped into a wall. We were slammed backward, landing on our butts. It took me a moment to realize what had happened.

"What the hell is going on?" Nicolas asked. He reached over and helped me to my feet.

I shook my head. "I don't know. It was like we hit a wall."

Nicolas narrowed his eyes. "I know this spell. Giovanni cast a spell blocking us from going forward."

Okay, now I was really angry. Who the hell did he think he was? We tried to move forward again, but the invisible barrier stopped us once again. It knocked the air out of my lungs each time I tried to break through.

"Maybe if we try to go through at the same time and hold hands," Nicolas said.

I nodded. "It's worth a shot."

Nicolas and I moved forward one more time. But we were thrown back again. I shook my head and tried to get over the shock. It knocked energy out of me each time we tried.

"Maybe we should go back. I want to get the car and drive over and check on my neighbor. I don't want

Giovanni messing with her because I'm sure he went to over there."

Nicolas grabbed my hand and we made our way across the area again, careful of our footing and watching for the fallen branches. We reached the other side and just as we stepped on the edge, we were knocked back again, falling to the ground. It was as if a bubble had captured us.

Panic surged through me. I felt trapped. How would we get out of here and what was Giovanni planning to do to us? I jumped up in a panic and moved forward again, sure that I could break through this time. It didn't happen though because I landed on the ground again. I was going to have some serious bruises. If I got a hold of Giovanni again I wasn't going to let him get by with this.

As I moved forward again, determined to break through no matter how many times it took, I fell back, stumbling and trying to remain upright. Nicolas reached to grab me before I hit the ground. But before he could save me, he lost his footing too, and landed near me. I let out a groan.

Nicolas moved closer and looked into my eyes. "Are you okay?"

My head was pounding and my body ached. I wasn't sure how many more times I could try to break through that barrier.

I rubbed my head. "I think I'm okay."

Nicolas inched closer and wrapped his arms around me, looking into my eyes. "Don't worry. I'll get us out of here," he whispered.

The sound of branches falling echoed around us and my heart pounded. I wasn't sure if it was because of the dire situation we were in or the look in Nicolas' eyes and his nearness. He leaned down and pressed his lips against mine. My tension eased and I felt comforted just knowing that we were in this together. If he said he would get us out of there, then I knew he meant it. He eased away and helped me up.

"We need to use magic to break through this. It's the only way out," Nicolas said.

My magic was drained and I didn't think I could push forward any longer.

Nicolas and I held hands to use each other's energy. To break the spell that had us captured, we'd call to the elements. Facing north, we recited the words: "Element of Earth, we call to you. Empower us with your energy to break free." We turned to face the west, and recited the words: "Element of Air, we call to you to push away the negative that entraps us." We shifted to face the south and recited the words: "Element of Fire, we call to you for protection and strength. Help us break free." Completing the spell, we moved again to face the east and recited the words: "Element of Water, we call to you for force and guidance. Give us the force to break the obstacle that's blocking us."

When the energy from the spell began to fade, another blast of wind stirred. The foreboding feeling swirled within the wind. Little by little the wind carried the foreboding feeling away. Finally the magic around us disappeared and I knew that the barrier had been broken.

I'd never felt more trapped in my whole life and I wasn't going to let Giovanni get away with that. Nicolas and I held hands and rushed out from the trees surrounding us. This time nothing stopped us.

After we got out of the magic barrier, we headed over to check on my neighbor. She was extremely unhappy with me when we showed up in the middle of the night, but at least I knew that she was safe and Giovanni hadn't paid her a visit.

CHAPTER TWENTY-SIX

A couple days had passed and there had been no sign of Giovanni or Kelley. My mother had wanted to hold a witches' festival for the longest time. Normally no one could ever get the licenses needed from the Enchantment Pointe Coven, but after I'd found Misty with Giovanni, she owed me.

My mother had wasted little time getting this festival together. I thought she would at least wait a month or two in order to get everything organized. But she just used her magic to whip it all up in two days. There would be crafts, food, games, and presentations on new spells and potions. Many vendors had set up booths with everything from amulets to magic-laced cupcakes.

Since fall was in full swing it was the perfect time for a festival. Winter would be here soon and my mother would be busy filling orders for the holidays. Enchantment Pointe and the shops in the historic section of town were a big holiday shopping destination for many towns away. My mother made special scents for the holidays that smelled of baked goods. But today was all about the witch festival and I was going to enjoy my time with Nicolas. There was nothing I could do about Giovanni at the moment, so I might as well try to enjoy myself.

Nicolas and I were checking out the different attractions, walking by the tables set up around town. I wanted to stop off for one of the new red velvet funnel cakes. Annabelle and Jon were walking around somewhere and I needed to meet up with them soon.

Nicolas picked up a silver bracelet and held it around my wrist. "This would look great on you."

I looked down at the silver bracelet with red stones. "It's beautiful."

Nicolas motioned for the woman behind the table. He handed her the cash, then fastened the bracelet around my wrist. He leaned down and kissed me.

"Thank you. It's lovely."

We stepped away from the table and continued to the sidewalk. I was enjoying the leisurely pace. It was hard to push the thoughts to the back of my mind, but I was trying my best not to think about all that was happening.

When I looked out in front of me over the crowd, I spotted Kelley up ahead. She was speaking with a woman at a table. I really wanted to know what she was saying. "Hey. There's Kelley. I want to confront her."

Nicolas frowned. "You're supposed to enjoy yourself today and not be stressed."

I looked at him for a second. "I won't let her stress me, I promise."

He nodded. "Yeah, right."

I grabbed his hand and we headed out across the crowd at a brisk pace. We weaved through the crowd and around the funnel cake stand. I tried to keep my eye on Kelley, but it was hard with all the people walking in front of us.

When I finally got around a group of witches wearing costumes with big black hats—for a moment I thought it was the coven—I looked at the table where I'd spotted Kelley. "She's gone," I said.

Nicolas and I looked around the crowd, but I didn't spot her anywhere. She could have easily blended in with the crowd and I'd never notice her again. Nevertheless, I wanted to talk with the woman she'd been talking to. Maybe she could tell me where Kelley had gone.

We hurried over to the table. A couple of people were speaking with the woman about some of her items. I made eye contact and I think she sensed right away that I was in a hurry. I pretended to look at some of her items as I moved anxiously beside the table. Finally the people walked away and the woman approached.

"May I help you?" Bright red lipstick covered her full lips and she offered a half-hearted smile. .

I nodded. "There was a woman talking with you just a few minutes ago. Do you know where she went?"

She shook her head. Her dark hair swung from side to side with the motion.

"You don't even know who I'm talking about yet. How can you shake your head that you don't know?"

She stared at me for a moment, then said in a curt tone, "Who is this woman?"

Why such hostility? "She's about twenty-five with pretty long dark hair. She was wearing a white blouse and jeans. She was just standing here a couple minutes ago," I said.

The woman frowned as if she didn't know what I was talking about.

"Come on, Hallie. Let's get out of here," Nicolas said, grabbing my arm.

A strange look crossed the woman's face. "Are you Halloween LaVeau?" she asked with wide eyes.

"Yes, I'm Hallie LaVeau."

"You're the new leader of the Underworld?"

I nodded. "Yes, and who are you?"

"I'm Eva David. I'm from the next town over." She kept busy moving items around her table, mostly avoiding my stare.

ROSE

I asked again, "Do you know where the woman went?"

"Well, there was a woman here. I didn't want to share this information with a stranger, you know. You can never be too careful," she said with a faint smile.

I smiled briefly. "I understand. What was she looking at?"

The woman looked down and grabbed a book. "She purchased a copy of this spellbook."

"Do you know this woman?" I asked.

She shook her head no, but I couldn't read her expression to know if she was telling the truth.

I took the book from her outstretched hand. The book had a black cover with gold letters on the front. I flipped it open. At first glance the spell book looked innocent enough, but at the back there were spells that could be used for black magic. Of course there was a disclaimer not to perform the spells, but what were they doing in the book if they didn't want anyone to perform them?

The woman must have noticed which spells I was looking at because she said, "Those spells are for entertainment only."

Yeah, right. I handed the book back to her. "Thank you for the help," I said.

She nodded with a little smile. "Sorry I couldn't help more. Please come back any time."

I started to turn around, but stopped. "How much is the book?" I asked.

"It's fifty dollars," she said.

"I'll take one," I said, grabbing my purse.

She waved her hands through the air. "Oh no, it's no charge for you. Think of it as a gift from me."

I shook my head. "That is very nice of you, but I'd rather just pay for it."

She frowned. "Really, I'd like for you to have it."

I sighed. "Well, okay, that is very nice of you. Thank you."

"Would you like me to put it in a bag for you?" she asked.

I waved my hand. "No, thank you. I'll just carry it like this."

She reached out and touched my arm. "I think it would be better if you put it in a bag."

I studied her face. Apparently she was completely serious about this. I nodded. "Okay, if you say so."

She reached down and grabbed a brown gift bag and placed the book inside with some white tissue paper. She handed the book back to me. "Enjoy."

"Thank you again," I said, holding the bag up.

"That was an odd exchange," Nicolas said as we walked away.

"Yeah, she didn't want me to carry the book without the bag, I wonder why."

He shook his head. "I don't know. It's another strange thing to add to the list of many strange things going on lately."

Nicolas and I walked away from the table. When I looked back, the woman was staring at me. She was probably lying for Kelley, but I had no way to prove it, right? I could try a spell to get her to tell the truth, but if I was going to all that trouble, then I should just try a spell that would lead me to Kelley. Which, now that I thought about it, was exactly what I was going to do. Why did it take me forever to think of these things? I'd save myself a whole lot of trouble if I could just get my act together.

But if I was going to do this, I needed a place away from all the witches to cast the spell. If I tried it with all of them around, not only would they sense my magic, but if it went like most of my spells, it would have negative effects on all other witches for miles around.

"I need to cast a spell to find Kelley," I said, as we walked along the sidewalk.

"Here?" Nicolas looked around. Even he knew what that would cause.

I shook my head. "No, we need to go somewhere quiet."

He concentrated for a moment, then said, "How about the park? Everyone is probably here at the festival and it should be almost empty."

"Sounds good. Let's go." I grabbed his hand.

"What about the book?" Nicolas asked when we reached the park.

A squirrel skipped across the green lawn and stopped by a nearby tree to nibble on his found treasure. A stone fountain bubbled in middle of the space. It had a paved pathway around it with benches and picnic tables just beyond the area.

"What about it?" I asked, putting the bag down on the picnic table.

"Is there a spell that you can cast from the book?"

I looked at him. "I hadn't thought about that, but maybe there is a good spell."

Since the book contained black magic, I had to be careful. One wrong move and it could be catastrophic.

I pulled the book from the bag and checked the index. "There's a spell to find something that you've lost."

"Well, you've lost Kelley, so I think that would work," he said.

I nodded. "Yeah, let's give it a try."

I flipped to the page listed in the table of contents. Luckily, it was a pretty straightforward spell and would only require words and our energy.

"Let's hold hands," I said.

Nicolas reached for my hands. His touch was warm and comforting. I looked into his eyes and began reciting the spell's words.

There was something different about this spell and I didn't know quite what to expect. There was no wind or feel of magic. I didn't even know if it was actually working. There were no flashes of light to let me know there was magic in action. Nicolas' grasp on my hands was strong and if I felt anything at all it was energy coming from him. I added extra words to the spell. It was the way that I performed spells—right or wrong, it was my way and I couldn't stop it.

Just when I thought it wasn't working, a light began to flash. It blinked off and on as if a television was trying to come into focus.

"Are you seeing that too?" Nicolas whispered.

I nodded. "Yeah, that's strange."

We continued to recite the words and the lights continued to flash. When the light grew so blindingly intense, it faded and that was when we saw her. A vision of Kelley appeared before us, like watching a movie. It showed her in a kitchen.

I looked at Nicolas and he shrugged. "Is that where she is?" I asked.

"It looked that way, yes," Nicolas said.

Kelley was in the kitchen with a small child and they were baking cookies. She didn't seem like the domestic type.

"It doesn't make sense. We just saw her here at the festival," I said.

The front of the house came into view with the number on the mailbox, then the street sign gave us a view of the street name. Nicolas and I exchanged a look.

"Are you ready to go there?" he asked.

"It's now or never," I said.

I picked up the book and we headed out of the park toward his car. Once in the car, I punched in the address on the GPS and we took off. Luckily, the street wasn't far away so we were there within a few minutes. There was a problem with the address though—the house was abandoned.

"What do we do now?" I asked.

"How about checking with the neighbor?" He pointed at the house next door.

"It's worth a shot," I said.

Nicolas and I walked up to the door, but I was sure that we were way off track. He rang the doorbell and we waited a few seconds until the door opened. A woman who I didn't recognize stood in front of us. It looked like the spell had been off track after all. I looked over at the address and looked back at the woman. Nicolas stood beside me.

The woman looked at us with a blank stare. She quirked an eyebrow and finally asked, "May I help you?"

By the scowl on her face, I knew she was angry that we were there. Had the spell led me here on purpose? That wouldn't surprise me. Kelley was all about playing games.

"Sorry to bother you, but do you know about the house over there?" I asked. Nicolas stared at her with his arms crossed in front of his chest waiting for her to answer.

She scowled. "No one lives there if that's what you're asking."

I looked her up and down. "I kind of figured that. Do you know who used to live there?"

She shrugged. I knew she was completely bored with this conversation. "A witch used to live there a long time ago."

"Do you know her name?" Nicolas asked.

She waved her hand. "Like I said, it's been a long time ago. I might have heard her name was Kelley."

The spell had been somewhat accurate, just off in the time period.

"Is there anything else you remember about her?" I asked.

She paused, then said, "I heard she was some important person in the witch world. I don't remember what you call it."

"The Underworld?" I asked.

She nodded. "Yeah, I guess that was it. Look, I have to go now."

When I looked at Nicolas, I knew he had the same thought. "I'm sorry that we bothered you."

Her expression eased. "That's okay. Sorry I couldn't help more."

"Thanks anyway," I said.

As we walked back to his car, I said, "We have to find out who Kelley really is."

We pulled out onto the street and I looked at the abandoned house as we drove by. I wondered what was in the book that made Kelley want it.

"Now where do we go from here?" Nicolas asked.

I peered out the window and watched the passing scenery, contemplating what I should say. Where did we go from here?

I tapped my fingers against the seat. "I guess we have to go back to the manor."

Nicolas made a U-turn and headed back in the direction of the festival. "We have to go back to the festival and ask the woman more questions. I'm not leaving until that woman tells us," he said as he steered the wheel.

By the time we made it back to the festival, the crowd had thinned. We jumped out of the car and rushed toward the booth. When we neared the area where the woman had been, my stomach sank. The table was gone and so was the woman.

CHAPTER TWENTY-SEVEN

The next morning, I had to do something to help figure out who Giovanni and Kelley were and what they wanted. Unfortunately that something involved another trip down into that creepy basement of the library.

I parked on the street in front of the library and marched inside as soon as they opened. After making my way through the main section, I inched down the dimly lit stairs and sprinted for the door that led to the little private room. If anyone saw me they'd think I was nuts. The faster I got in there, the faster I could get out. I wasn't even sure what I was looking for, but I didn't know what else to do. I scanned the row for the book on the coven members. Since I'd seen the symbol again on what was supposedly Giovanni's item, I had to look for more information.

I placed the book on the table and aimlessly flipped through the pages. Nothing looked remotely interesting. It was mostly talk about the coven's spells and cooking. There was no mention about how bad they were at witchcraft. I never thought I'd meet any witches who were worse at casting spells than me, but I'd finally met my match.

I flipped the old pages and my hand froze when I reached a page at the back of the book. How had I missed this information earlier? Apparently the symbol that the witches used in 1785 was also used by the coven in 1885 and 1985. Was it a coincidence that Kelley knew about the symbol and she came back from the 1980s? What did the coven members know about this? How would I find out if Kelley was being truthful? I'd been fooled by reanimated spirits before, but now it was just getting ridiculous. Fool me once, shame on you. Fool me twice, shame on me. But fool me three times and it was time to kick some butt.

Making my way over to the section marked 1985, I pulled the book from the shelf and carried it over to the table. After searching through the book, there was no mention of Giovanni's mother. As a matter of fact, the pages had been ripped from the book. I knew that was no coincidence.

I had to find out what the symbol meant and where it came from. Was it the key to Giovanni's ability to cast a spell and add it to the book? Had he used that symbol to his advantage and it had allowed him to add spells to the book? But the coven members used this symbol and their spells were dreadful at times, so I wasn't sure what the symbol would do for him.

Did the coven members know more information about what the symbol stood for and why they'd had it in the first place? According to the book, each coven had a symbol that held some special meaning. Now that I thought about it, Enchantment Pointe had a symbol. It had been the same for many years. And to be honest, I'd always thought it held no special powers other than being a symbol to distinguish our coven from the others.

With the information in hand, I made it back up those creepy stairs, almost tripping at the top I moved so quickly. I had to get back to the manor. What was I going to say to the coven? Maybe I needed to cast a spell that would make them more likely to be honest with me.

It seemed to take forever to get back to the manor. My stomach was in knots knowing that I had to confront the coven and Kelley. I released a deep breath and hurried up the front steps. I should have probably waited for Nicolas before confronting them, but I knew I wouldn't be able to wait.

When I raced through the door, I stormed through and made my way to the parlor. The coven members stopped in midair. They were literally floating off the floor.

"Get down from there," I yelled. "What the hell are you doing now?"

"We were just working on our spells," Barbara said.

"No more! You're not going to practice magic here. You all are terrible, worse than I ever imagined. I want to know what you know about the symbol. I found out that it's used for the years 1785, 1885, and 1985." I held up the pouch. "You all need to be honest with me. I thought we were friends?"

The women floated to the floor.

"Yes, that is our symbol, but we don't know anything about it being used for other years or covens. And that's the truth," Rebecca said with a glare.

The women nodded and stared at me with frowns on their faces. Apparently they were upset with me, but I didn't care at the moment. I'd been tricked one too many times.

"You say you don't have any information about Giovanni? I don't believe you," I said.

Rebecca looked shocked that I would say such a thing. I crossed my arms in front of my chest and waited for them to tell me the truth. One by one they walked out of the room and headed upstairs. I supposed they were going to their rooms like sulking eight-year-olds. They could pout if they wanted, but I didn't believe that it was a coincidence that the symbol had been mentioned in the book about their coven.

Since I couldn't get hold of Nicolas or Liam, I decided to go to Bewitching Potions and talk to my mother about what was happening. I hopped in the car again and made my way downtown.

As I was walking down the sidewalk, I bumped into Constance Newton. She owned the bakery next door to my mother's shop. She'd always been nice despite the fact that I'd accidentally almost burned down her store a couple years ago. This was the bakery where I'd taken the witches. Luckily Constance hadn't been working that day and didn't know that I'd been outside her shop again.

"Hello, Hallie. It's nice to see you again." She gave me that familiar pitying look that I'd grown accustomed to from Enchantment Pointe residents.

"Hi, Ms. Newton. How's the baking?" I asked.

She smiled. "Great."

I knew she didn't want me to stop in her store. I normally walked the long way to my mother's shop just to avoid walking past her bakery.

"I saw you with a young woman yesterday. She looked just like somebody I knew a long time ago. What's her name?" she asked.

"Her name is Kelley Killebrew," I said.

She frowned. "That's right. I remember her now. She lived in Fern Creek."

"What do you remember about her?" I asked.

She looked at my face and said, "She was the leader of the Underworld."

My stomach dropped and for a moment I was speechless. This was definitely a twist that I hadn't expected. So that was what the woman had meant when she said Kelley was a higher-up in the Underworld.

"She died in a car accident," Constance added before I had a chance to respond.

So that much had been true. No wonder her magic had been so good.

177

Constance continued, "But she'd been stripped of her leadership status right before she died. If I remember correctly, your great-aunt had something to do with her status being revoked."

Slowly this was all started to make sense, but I still had to fit together all the pieces.

"Do you have any more information about her?" I asked.

"She has an aunt who still lives in Fern Creek. Maybe she could be of more help to you. I believe she lives on Emerald Street," she said.

After jotting down the address, I said, "Thank you for the information. I have to go." I rushed away and pulled out my cell phone.

I didn't want to make this trip alone.

CHAPTER TWENTY-EIGHT

Annabelle had met me at Bewitching Potions. My mother popped up from behind the counter when we walked in the door. "Oh, am I glad to see you all. I need some help." She looked at Annabelle.

My mother had given up on me doing the spells correctly and had turned her attention to Annabelle. I would be jealous, but I knew I couldn't do it, so why not let Annabelle have the pleasure of doing these crazy spells with my mother?

Annabelle shook her head. "Tell me what I need to do."

"You know what to do," my mother said.

Without saying a word, Annabelle hurried around the room gathering bottles and potions from the shelves. She had all the stuff she needed for a spell. I watched as she moved easily around the room.

She placed the stuff on the counter then blew the hair out of her eyes. "Okay, how's that? Did I get everything?"

My mother smiled. "I can't believe what a natural knack you have for this."

She looked at me and I shrugged. "She's a natural."

Annabelle smiled. I still couldn't believe that she was actually agreeing to this. She placed all the ingredients in the cauldron and began stirring the concoction.

"Do you want to help recite the words?" my mother asked.

I pointed at my chest. "Who, me?" I shook my head. "No way. This is all on you all. If it goes wrong, I don't want to be held responsible."

My mother shrugged. "Suit yourself."

I watched as they continued. The pot bubbled at just the right moments.

"I think it's working," Annabelle said with wide eyes and giddiness.

I laughed. "Yeah."

I hated to say this, but I didn't want to be the one to test out this potion that she had just made. My mother could try it. The bubbles died down and my mother decanted some of the potion into a brown bottle. She slapped a label on the front. "Here you go, Hallie, test it out and see how it works."

I shook my head. "No way."

Annabelle placed her hands on her hips. "You don't trust my potion-making powers?"

I looked at her. "Would you trust mine?"

She studied my face for a moment, then chuckled. "No, I wouldn't."

"Thank you," I said.

My mother grabbed the bottle. "Fine, I'll try it. I'm used to trying the stuff Hallie does, how much worse could it be?"

***

I hadn't wanted to wait around to see if the spell actually worked. Besides, with beauty potions, sometimes it was days or weeks before it took effect. A few minutes after leaving my mother's shop, Annabelle and I hurried along the sidewalk. "This not being able to call you thing is getting out of control. I hate it."

"Are you ready for a short road trip?" I asked.

"Something tells me we're not going to the beach." Her tone was teasing, but I knew she was worried all the same.

I snorted. "I wish. No, we're not going to the beach. We need to talk with a woman in Fern Creek."

"This has something to do with the paranormal, huh?" she asked.

"Doesn't it always?" I asked as I motioned for her to follow me back to my car.

We pointed the car south and headed out on a mission. Fern Creek was the next town over from Enchantment Pointe. There really was nothing there, so I hadn't been many times. I'd had a friend who was dating a guy from there. They'd eventually got married and moved away. Now I never had a reason to go there. That was until today.

I was anxious about what I would discover. Maybe Ms. Newton had no idea what she was talking about. That would be a little embarrassing to say the least if I approached Kelley's aunt and she had no clue what I meant. I was tired of being lied to by these spirits though and I had to track down any detail I discovered. Couldn't one of the spirits be honest for a change? I'd thought I could trust Kelley.

We drove around town for twenty minutes looking for the street, but it was like it didn't exist. Finally, I pulled up in front of the diner. "We should go in and ask if anyone knows this woman. People in small-town diners always know where to find people."

"You've been watching too many movies," she said.

"Actually, we haven't watched nearly enough lately. I miss our movie nights," I said as we neared the diner.

"Ever since you moved into the manor," she said with a sigh.

When we stepped inside the place it went silent. Forks and coffee mugs were frozen in midair. Apparently they didn't see strangers often. The smell of French fries and burnt meat lingered in the air. We sat at the counter and waited for the waitress to finally come over.

She wiped a glitter of sweat from her forehead with a towel and then blew her red bangs out of her eyes. "What can I get you for ladies?"

She handed us the menu and I said, "Oh, we don't need a menu. We're actually looking for someone."

"You didn't come here to eat anything?" she asked with a frown.

"Well, actually…" I said.

"We would love to order something," Annabelle said, grabbing the menu and winking at me.

***

If it hadn't been for Annabelle complimenting the waitress on her great hair, I doubt we would have gotten the right address. Annabelle always had a way with people.

With the correct address in hand, we made our way according to the directions.

"It will be a miracle if this actually takes us there," I said.

We made a couple right turns and then a left. Annabelle counted down until we reached the correctly numbered mailbox. It was a gravel driveway that was overgrown with brush.

"I don't like the looks of this place," Annabelle gripped the side of the seat as if holding on for life.

I knew as soon as I saw how creepy it looked that Annabelle would want to end this trip. We pulled down the long driveway and the old farmhouse came in to view.

There were more overgrown trees surrounding the house. The house looked like it had needed painting about ten years ago. The porch squeaked under our feet.

"I hope this thing doesn't collapse with us standing on it," Annabelle said, looking down at the rickety floorboards.

I knocked on the door and immediately heard shuffling from the other side. Annabelle looked at me with a horrified expression.

The door inched open. "What do you want?" the old woman asked, glaring at us with her deep green eyes. Her gray hair had come undone from its bun and her beige floral dress was incorrectly buttoned down the front. The wrinkles on her face deepened with her frown.

"Um, we're sorry for bothering you. We're looking for someone by the name of Kelley Killebrew."

A deathly pallor fell across her face. There was something odd about this woman. Magical energy surrounded her. It wasn't coming from me, and I knew it wasn't coming from Annabelle, so it had to be her or someone else was in the house. I looked over her shoulder into the dimly lit space. With sparse furnishings and untidiness, it almost looked as if the house was abandoned.

"Are you a witch?" I asked.

She narrowed her eyes at me. "What business is that of yours?"

"I'm the leader of the Underworld," I said.

As soon as I mentioned that I was the leader, she opened the door wide. "I'm sorry, my hearing isn't what it used to be. Did you ask if I was a witch?" She held her hand up to her ear.

I nodded. "Yes, that's what I asked."

"Why yes, dear, I am. What can I do for you?" Her voice now dripped with honey and her demeanor had changed completely.

"My name is Hallie LaVeau and this is Annabelle Preston." I looked at her expectantly and she finally followed my lead.

"I'm Patricia Killebrew. Would you like to come inside?"

"This is creepy," Annabelle whispered.

I expected Annabelle to retreat to the car at any moment. We stepped inside the house.

"Won't you please have a seat?" She motioned around the room. The sofa and chairs were covered with stacks of newspapers. "Oh, let me move that for you," she said as she scooped up the papers.

Annabelle and I eased down on the edge of the sofa cushions. Annabelle's eyes were wide as she looked around the room.

I leaned forward and fixed my gaze on the woman. "Like I said, we hate to bother you, but do you know Kelley Killebrew?"

Patricia lowered her head, then looked up at us. "She was my niece."

"Was she the leader of the Underworld?" I asked.

She hesitated, but finally nodded. "Yes, she was until…"

"Until she passed away?" I asked.

Patricia nodded, but didn't speak. She stood up from the chair and shuffled over to a cabinet across the room.

"Would she have any reason to come back in spirit?" I asked.

Patricia looked at me with a scowl. "No," she said sharply. "What's done is done."

"Was she stripped of her leadership status before she died?" I pressed.

"Just because you're the leader doesn't mean I have to tell you anything," she said.

I nodded. "No, you don't have to, but it would be a great help if you did."

Patricia paused, then said. "She was misunderstood, that's all. She wanted some witches removed, but they were bad witches."

"Who were the witches?" I asked.

"I don't have to tell you anything else," she said.

Patricia pulled out a silver picture frame and moved back over to us. She held out the frame and we looked down at the picture.

Annabelle released a little gasp and I squeezed her hand. It was exactly what I had expected. Constance had been telling the truth. The woman in the picture had the same brown eyes and dark shiny hair—the same bright smile. It was Kelley and apparently she had been the leader of the Underworld.

CHAPTER TWENTY-NINE

After getting little information, we headed back to LaVeau Manor to see if Kelley was there. If she was, then I had to confront her. Why had she lied? Was she connected with Giovanni? She'd done an excellent job of tricking me. I'd thought she was a sweet girl. Now it turned out that I couldn't trust her at all. I had no idea what her true motives were.

"I can't believe what we found out," Annabelle said in a shaky voice.

I shook my head. "I can't believe I trusted her."

We parked in front of the manor and rushed up the steps and through the front door. Luckily, the women weren't casting any spells at the moment. We ran up the stairs to Kelley's room, but she wasn't there. The front door opened and closed. Annabelle and I exchanged a look and hurried down the stairs.

I was relieved to see that it was Nicolas. "Are you okay?" he asked as he rushed over to me. "You look like something's wrong."

Before I had a chance to tell Nicolas about what had happened, my phone rang and I knew it wasn't going to be good news when I saw Liam's number displayed on the screen.

"Hallie, what's going on there?" he asked in a panicked voice. I'd never heard him like that before.

"I was looking for Kelley, have you seen her?" I asked.

"Yes, I've seen her. She's here. I need you to come here right away." Tension reverberated through Liam's voice.

"What's wrong, Liam?" I asked.

Nicolas stepped closer with a concerned look on his face.

"Just get to the plantation as soon as you…"

The phone went dead.

"Liam? Liam?"

There was no answer.

"What happened?" Nicolas asked.

"The phone went dead, but he wants us to come to the plantation as soon as possible. Kelley is there."

"Oh, this doesn't sound good," Annabelle said.

"Annabelle, I don't want you to have to deal with this," I said.

She shook her head. "I'm your best friend and I won't leave you to deal with this alone."

"I have Nicolas to go with me."

"Well, you guys might need help. I'm going with you," she said.

CHAPTER THIRTY

We jumped in the car and headed toward the plantation. Tension filled the air. If not for Nicolas' soothing presence, I don't know what I would have done. Would Giovanni pop up behind us again? I had no idea what to expect when I got to the plantation. I'd dealt with a lot of weird stuff over the past few weeks, but I didn't want to deal with another demon. I just hoped that Liam was okay.

I glanced back at Annabelle. She had a worried expression on her face. "Are you okay?"

She nodded, but I knew by the look on her face that she was anything but okay.

Nicolas looked ahead, focusing his attention on the road in front of us. The sun would be setting soon and I hoped to get to the plantation before darkness fell. I glanced over at the speedometer.

Nicolas noticed and said, "It's probably not safe to drive any faster. This back road has a lot of curves."

I nodded. Of course he was right, but that didn't make the situation any less stressful. Annabelle fidgeted in the back seat and I knew her stress level was at an all-time high.

THIRD TIME'S A

Finally, we approached the turnoff for the plantation and made our way down the long gravel drive. The sun melted, spilling color over the western sky. Darkness was waiting for me. The house seemed so peaceful and quiet. There was no noise and I didn't see anyone.

"It looks like no one is home," Annabelle said as she walked beside me.

She looked like she was in ready-to-run mode. The slightest noise might send her running away from this place and I couldn't say that I blamed her. I might run too if I could. Since I was still the leader I had an obligation to take care of this.

We stepped up the front porch and I turned the knob. After the last conversation with Liam I wasn't going to bother to knock or ring the doorbell. I was pretty sure he was expecting me.

I called out to him. "Liam? Where are you?"

No one answered and there was no sound from inside the house. The longer we went without finding him the worse I felt. My stomach was twisted into a knot.

"I'll check upstairs and you all can check down here," Nicolas said as he climbed the stairs two at a time.

Annabelle and I didn't split up to find Liam. There was no way she was leaving my side and frankly I didn't want her to leave me either. If something had happened to Liam, I didn't want to confront Kelley alone.

We searched all of the downstairs and finally came back around to the foyer. Nicolas was just coming down the stairs when we entered.

"They're not up there," Nicolas said as he approached.

I shook my head. "They're not down here either."

"We should check outside," he said, making his way to the front door.

Annabelle and I followed. I stepped out into the yard and looked around, but I saw nothing. Not even the leaves on the trees were swaying. I'd never seen it so still out here before. There was usually at least some wind.

"You all go around that side and I'll go around this side of the house. We can meet at the back," Nicolas said.

Annabelle and I took off around the side of the house.

"Do you feel eyes on us? Why is it so quiet here?" Though her words were spoken softly there was an underlying sense of panic.

I shook my head. "I don't know." I didn't mention to her that it was freaking me out.

Annabelle and I made it around the side of the house and I was almost expecting something or someone to jump out at us. The air surrounding the plantation had turned suddenly creepy and a little ominous. I knew that meant magic was in motion. Or at least it was very near.

When we made it to the back of the house, I spotted Nicolas walking toward us.

"Did you see them?" Nicolas asked.

I nodded. "They're not out here either."

"They must have left," he said.

"I don't like the way this is going. Do you notice the change in the air?" I asked.

He nodded and a look of concern spread across this face. "Yes, I noticed it as I was coming around the house."

That was the same time I'd felt it. Heck, even Annabelle had felt it and she'd always been oblivious to the paranormal.

A noise echoed through the air and we looked at each other. "Where did that come from?" I asked.

"It sounded like it was at the front of the house," Nicolas said.

We hurried around to the front of the house. Liam and Kelley were together, getting into his car. They didn't look up and I didn't think they had noticed us.

"Stop right there," Nicolas said. His voice carried, loud and authoritative, across the air.

Liam and Kelley turned around to look at us at the same time. Where had they been? It looked as if they were getting in to the car to leave, not as if they'd just arrived.

Kelley frowned and Liam looked around as if he was planning his next move. She didn't answer, but I knew she had no intention of stopping unless we forced her.

Nicolas yelled at Kelley again as he rushed toward the car. I ran behind him.

Liam ran over to us. "Kelley was forcing me to drive her to find Giovanni and then she wanted to find you."

Kelley lifted her arm and whirled it around, then pointed it at Nicolas. An evil smile spread across her face when the energy hit Nicolas and kicked him to the ground. I ran over to him, but the spell she'd just cast was keeping me away. She zapped him with the spell again when he tried to get up. Why hit him twice? Wasn't it enough that she'd already sent him to the ground? I had to prepare myself for what would happen next. I knew she would use her magic on me next.

I ran through the spells in my mind, trying to figure out which one I would use to stop her. My mind was blank and I couldn't think of anything that would help. She reached her arms into the air again and I knew she was focusing her energy on me this time. A whirling wind circled around her as if fueling her power. She narrowed her eyes and focused her dark stare on me, but before she could cast the spell, Giovanni and Kevin drove up.

The black car came to a stop and they jumped out. Had they followed us here? Kelley lowered her arms. The spell had been paused for the moment, but I knew that she wouldn't give up that easily.

Giovanni and Kevin stepped closer and stood beside Kelley. I should have known they were in on this together. That was why they had the symbol.

Giovanni stood tall and puffed out his chest. "I demand that you give me the book now or I will have to kill you and all your little friends."

I stood my ground. "There is no way in hell you are getting the book. Give up your little fantasy."

Nicolas finally managed to break free from the spell that Kelley had cast and joined me. My mind was still blank on what spell I should try on this evil bunch. Before I had a chance to even wave my arm to try a spell, Giovanni lifted his arms and pointed them at us. I knew what was about to come our way and it wasn't going to feel good. Wind whirled around him and a dark mass circled around his head. It traveled down and then carried across the air until it smacked us head on. We immediately fell to the ground.

As if an invisible force lifted us from the ground, we began walking. Nicolas, Liam, Annabelle, and I headed toward the plantation. We moved up the front steps toward the front door. I looked back and Kelley and Giovanni were laughing. We were powerless to stop whatever force was making us move inside the house. We moved inside the house and the large wooden door slammed shut behind us. This spell and evil energy had banished us inside the plantation.

As soon as the door slammed shut, we were able to move of our own free will again. I ran to the door and twisted the knob, but it wouldn't budge.

"Stand back." Nicolas warned with a wave of his arm.

Liam and Nicolas pulled on the door, but it wouldn't open.

"We'll try the back door," Liam said with a firm no-nonsense voice.

Liam and Nicolas ran to the back, while Annabelle and I continued pulling on the door. I looked outside and saw Kelley and Giovanni talking. That same black mass was circling around their heads. I wasn't sure what it was, but I knew it was powerful. We had to find a way to get rid of the spell and get out of the house.

Nicolas and Liam ran from the back of the house, but I knew by their expressions that they hadn't gotten the doors to open back there either.

"We're going to break the front window," Liam said.

The words had just left his lips when a loud noise echoed from outside. We hurried over to the window. I couldn't believe my eyes. The coven members had pulled up in an old car. Where in the hell had they gotten the car from and how did they manage to drive it? I was pretty sure that they'd used their magic. They were just lucky that they hadn't wrecked on the way here.

"What are they doing here?"

Had they come to help Kelley, Kevin and Giovanni? After all, the symbol had originated from their coven. The front and back doors on the old jalopy opened at the same time and the women jumped out. We stared in silence, waiting to see what would happen next.

The women focused their attention on Giovanni and Kelley, who had stopped and were now staring at the women. The coven members grabbed hands and formed a semi-circle. The wind whirled around them and a cloud of mist burst up from the ground. They began a little dance, which any other time would have been quite comical. It was a scene that would have garnered a few million hits on YouTube if I'd recorded it.

The white cloud swooped forward and rushed toward Giovanni, Kevin and Kelley. They fell backward onto the ground, landing on their butts. They looked around in a dazed sort of confusion. At that moment the lock on the front door clicked and then it slowly swung open. I couldn't believe that the coven members had come here to help us. I still wasn't sure if they could be trusted though. They might have an agenda of their own.

Once the door opened, we hurried out of the house and down the front steps. Giovanni, Kevin and Kelley were still on the ground trying to make their way up.

Finally, Kelley, Kevin and Giovanni climbed to their feet. The white cloud had dissipated and without warning they ran toward their cars.

"They're trying to get away," Annabelle yelled.

They made it to the car and opened the doors before the coven members slammed them with another spell. It was quite funny to watch actually. That same white cloud engulfed their entire car.

"Whoa, how do they do that?" Annabelle whispered.

"It's magic," I said.

But she already knew that much. To be honest, I had no idea why their magic was so good now when it had been so bad before. I knew mine had improved because of the Book of Mystics, but why had they improved? Had they taken the Book of Mystics? It wouldn't surprise me if they had. Everyone wanted it.

I joined the circle with the women and we began reciting the spell. The white cloud circled us. It weaved in and out and around our legs. It climbed and weaved before finally hovering over us again. I couldn't believe that I had joined with the coven members to do a spell.

Would it really work? The other spell they had performed worked, so why not this one? Whatever had happened to them, I was glad it had worked because now more than ever I needed help. Our words grew louder and stronger and I felt the white energy around us.

The air around the plantation had been heavy, but the more we chanted the more it dissipated. Soon the heaviness lifted and I looked around. The white cloud above us had disappeared. Nicolas, Liam, and Annabelle looked out over the lawn at us from the front porch. To say that they looked tense would have been an understatement. Apparently, the spell that the coven members and I had cast had broken whatever spells Giovanni, Kevin and Kelley had placed around the plantation. We released hands and I felt the energy drain from my arms all the way down to my feet. It had taken all of the energy I had to cast the spell with them.

When I stepped around, Giovanni, Kevin and Kelley were nowhere in sight. I ran over to Nicolas.

"Where did they go?" I asked.

"When the spell was finished they walked off. They went that way through the lines of trees." He pointed.

Had they just disappeared? Would that be possible? I hadn't been sure of what would happen to them, but I hadn't expected for them to just walk away. Would they be back? For now the energy around us felt light and definitely didn't have that sinister feeling that Giovanni and Kelley had caused. I didn't know if it could be that easy to get rid of them though.

"Do you think they are gone?" Annabelle asked.

I shrugged. "It looks like it, but I don't know with them. I don't trust them."

The coven members climbed back in the car.

"Where are you going? I asked.

"We're going back to Enchantment Pointe." Rebecca cranked the engine and pulled out without giving me a chance to say thank you.

They really did need to go back to the other dimension though. Along with Kelley too, but it didn't look as if I was going to find her to do that. If only there was a spell that would let me do it without her being around.

We jumped back in the car and headed back to LaVeau Manor to see if Giovanni, Kevin and Kelley were there and to see if the coven was really going back there. Heck, for all I knew they might be headed to the Bubbling Cauldron for more dancing and drinks. If Giovanni, Kevin and Kelley were at the manor, then I had to get rid of them for good.

When we finally arrived back at the manor, the old jalopy that the coven had driven was parked in front. I still didn't know how they'd gotten the car. After the long drive we pulled up to the manor and I was thankful to see that the coven hadn't destroyed the place. I was afraid to find out what they'd done to the inside though.

We'd searched the manor, but had found no sign of Giovanni and company. It had been a long evening with little results. We'd have to try again tomorrow. It felt strange to think that Liam would be staying in the manor with me again. I was back to having both of the brothers at the manor. I couldn't seem to get away from that situation.

"Are you ready to go inside?" Nicolas chuckled.

"Not really," I said, "but I guess it's now or never."

After searching through the house, I discovered the women in their rooms. This was good because it would give me a chance to cast a spell without them. I would try to call Kelley back to the manor. If the witches knew what I was doing, they'd probably try to stop me.

It would have been better if I could have used my cauldron for the spell, but in a pinch I'd just have to try the spell without it. I didn't want them to step into the kitchen and catch me using the cauldron. Yes, it was mine to use, but it was easier to be stealthy this way. I grabbed the book and a spell appeared. I recited the words and used the various spices, sprinkling them around the room.

When the heavy energy was gone, I stepped out from the room and listened. I didn't hear any sound. Would Kelley appear soon? She had to sense that I was looking for her. I stepped through the house, practically holding my breath at what might happen next.

When I reached the doorway the witches were standing there staring at me.

"We know what you tried and it's very dangerous. You shouldn't provoke her." Rebecca placed her hands on her hips and glared at me. "It's a good thing you have us around."

"Giovanni and Kelley can't do anything," I said.

The women's eyes grew wide and they looked over my shoulder. I spun around and let out a gasp. The spell had worked. Kelley stood in the middle of the floor. She didn't look as perky now… her expression said it all. She was livid. The bow in her hair drooped to the left and her mascara was smeared down her cheeks.

"You thought you could get rid of us that easily. I am not happy." Kelley glared at me.

I threw my hands up. "Well, I am not happy either. Do you think I want you here?"

"Then why the hell don't you just hand over the book?" she demanded.

"You had plenty of chance to get the book. Why didn't you try to take it yourself?" I asked.

"You always had it in your hands," she said.

I smiled. "So you're not so tough after all."

She narrowed her eyes at me. "Don't be so sure. This isn't over yet. I've formed a new coven with Giovanni and Kevin. Or powers together will be too much for you."

Without warning, she turned around and walked off. I looked back at the coven members and they shrugged. I chased after Kelley. Where did she think she was going? I wasn't through with her. She had to be banished back to the other dimension.

CHAPTER THIRTY-ONE

I ran through the house after Kelley. Well, at least I thought I'd been chasing after her, but now I couldn't find her. I looked around the empty room. Where had she gone? Maybe I'd gotten lucky and the spell had worn off and she'd already gone back to the other dimension.

I moved back to the kitchen. The coven members weren't there either. I walked over to the back door and looked out, but didn't see them. What was with everyone disappearing?

I rushed down the hallway and checked the dining room, but there was no sign of Kelley there either. I knew she couldn't have walked past me when I was at the front of the house. She had to be outside. But maybe my spell had worked and had just taken a while to take effect. I couldn't count on that though, so I had to look for her.

I'd been correct. Kelley was standing in front of the manor. It was like she was waiting for me to come outside. She was waiting for this confrontation. If that was what she wanted, well, then that was what I would give her. I walked over to her, fully aware that our conversation could turn ugly at any moment. I doubted she wanted to be civil at a time like this.

She crossed her arms in front of her chest and glared at me. "You won't win this battle," she snapped.

I stared her dead in the eyes. "Are you partners with Giovanni? Did he send you here?"

She scoffed, but since her answer was delayed, I knew she had devised this plan with him.

"Why did you do this?" I asked.

Since she hadn't answered my other question, I was sure she wouldn't answer this one either. Would she admit that she had been the leader? She looked around and I wondered what her next move would be. The little wheels moving round and round were practically visible. What was she planning?

After a couple seconds, she looked at me and said, "Fine. You want to know what is going on? I'll tell you what's going on. I was looking for your precious great-aunt Madelyn."

"Why were you looking for her? There is nothing you can do to Aunt Maddy now. She's dead," I said.

Her eyes narrowed at the mere mention of Maddy's name. Kelley's posture tensed and her face scrunched up into an evil scowl. I stared at her, waiting for an answer. "First you need to know that I was a powerful witch in my day."

I looked at her. "In the Eighties, right?" I scoffed. "You could have fooled me because I heard you were nothing special. I know about you being the leader. Apparently you weren't a very good leader. That was why my great-aunt stopped you."

I wasn't sure about that fact, but I knew my great-aunt, and that was something she would have done.

She narrowed her eyes. "Yes, I was the leader. A better leader than you'd ever be. You're not good at any spells. None, zero, nada."

"What difference does that make?" I asked.

She smirked. "It means that I am more powerful than you think."

"Are you saying that to intimidate me?"

"Yes, I am."

She didn't take her focus off my face and I didn't falter either.

"Well, I've got news, it's not working," I said. "I don't understand what any of this has to do with me. Why did you come back?"

She shook her head. "Don't you see, when I discovered that your aunt was no longer with us, I had to come after the next best thing." She flashed that snide look again. "I decided that I wanted to go after Madelyn's relatives. And I wanted to be the leader again. When I found out you were the new leader, well, even more reason to take you down."

"I wouldn't be so sure of that if I were you."

"There is nothing you can do to me," she said.

"We'll see about that," I said.

The witches appeared beside me. Where had they been and how had they known to come now? That was probably something that would never be answered. I hoped they weren't joining forces with Kelley.

"What did Aunt Maddy do that was so terrible?"

Kelley shook her head. "Only the worst thing you could possibly do to a witch. She tried to strip me of my powers! She even threatened to have me burned at the stake."

A few of the coven members let out gasps. That was no joking matter.

I swallowed hard. "I don't believe you, and even if she did, she had a good reason. Based on what I've seen of your personality now, I'm guessing you did some pretty nasty things."

"There is no reason to take away a witch's powers."

"If she's bad, then there are a lot of reasons," I said.

"Regardless, thanks to you I was able to come back and take care of business."

Yeah, great. Kelley's spirit had managed to gain a human form from my spell. Big shocker there, huh?

"Well, thanks to me I am going to send you packing back to where you came from."

"I'm not going anywhere," she said, glaring at me. "I've had enough of the chitchat. I have to get Giovanni so we can get rid of you for good."

She was bold and not mincing words. That was fine, I could take her talk. "You're all talk and no action," I said.

Her face twisted into a scowl.

"How did Giovanni add spells to the Book of Mystics?" I asked.

"He's a brilliant man. He came up with a spell that made it look as if he'd added spells to the book."

"I'd have to disagree on how brilliant he is," I said.

"Giovanni's mother never added a spell, yet he made you think that she had. Don't you think that's brilliant?"

The fact that he'd pulled that off made me furious. It had all been a lie that he'd concocted in order to get the book. How long had he been working on this plan? Giovanni had added the first spell and then added one right in front of my eyes, so of course I'd believed it to be real. I was thankful that I'd discovered the truth before it was too late. It had been Kelley and Giovanni trying to fool me all along. It had worked for some time—I'd almost lost the book to him because of it. Thank goodness that hadn't happened.

"You didn't tell me what your connection to Giovanni is," I said. "Did he come back from the grave before you? Was he dead too?"

"Why don't you figure that out for yourself," she snapped.

"Because I'm demanding that you tell me now," I said.

"You can't demand me to tell you anything."

"I just did."

"Giovanni and I just met, if you must know," she said with a smirk.

"So why are you helping him? If you think he is going to help you then you are sadly wrong," I said.

Kelley had led me to believe that Giovanni had been the leader in 1985. That had been a sham, all part of her plan to lure me into a false sense of security, then she would bounce when the time was just right.

"Giovanni is a nice and compassionate man and I know he will help me any way that he can. He knows I am to be the true leader."

I chuckled. "So you've fallen for this guy? Wow, you're dumber than I thought you were. You know he wants to be the leader."

"He knows I need him to help me become the leader again, plus he'll help me get rid of you. That is my ultimate goal. It was a no-lose situation by helping him."

"You're wrong about that. You didn't achieve anything by helping him. Oh wait, I take that back. You managed to make me very angry. Congratulations on that," I said.

She stared a hole through me.

"Look, maybe if you stop this now I can be lenient on you."

"Thanks, that's so sweet of you, but I don't need any favors. Now, if you'll excuse me I have to get Giovanni and Kevin so that we can finish you off."

She turned around to leave and I called out to her, "Kelley, stop right there!"

I knew I was going to have to use magic to get her to stop. But just how powerful was she really? I was about to find out. I looked around at the coven members and they nodded. At least I knew I had their help.

We followed Kelley outside. I stopped at the bottom of the steps when I saw Kelley, Giovanni, Kevin and the woman from the Witches' Festival, Eva David.

"Hallie, I'd like you to meet my coven." Kelley waved her arms through the air, gesturing toward the others.

Now I knew that they hadn't been gone after all. I didn't want to have another battle with them, but it looked like they wouldn't give me any other options. I had to figure out how to get rid of them once and for all. There was only one thing I could do. I had to confront them.

"You're the woman from the festival. Why are you here? Why did you give me that spellbook?" I asked.

"You were supposed to do the black magic in the book and it would have backfired on you. Can't you do anything right?"

"So you set me up? If I'd done the black magic spells they would have hurt me?"

Eva smirked. "That was the plan."

"Well, it wasn't a very smart one. You shouldn't have left any good magic spells in the book if you'd wanted something bad to happen to me," I said.

"I didn't know you were going to show up at my booth. I had to think quickly and cast a spell on the spot. It's hard to do the silent spells with a victim standing right there. The longer you held the book in the bag, the worse the spells would have been for you."

No wonder she wanted me carry the book in a bag.

"I don't even know you why are you coming after me?" I asked.

"Kelley was my best friend. If she doesn't like you, then I don't like you," she said.

Would the 1785 coven members help me this time? No matter, I had to do this on my own. I was the leader and I could handle this.

"I'll be right back," I said as I ran past the 1785 coven members and back inside.

"Look at the little witch run," Kelley cackled.

I rushed up to my bedroom and dug the spellbook out of the locked trunk. I grabbed the heavy tome, tugged it under my arm and raced down the stairs. When I reached the bottom of the stairs, I knew that it wouldn't be a good idea to take the book outside with me.

I flipped open the cover and said, "Show me the spell to get rid of them."

As if following my command, the pages flipped. The wind blew and when it settled I peered down at the page. I could understand the words and they weren't in the weird language this time. I never knew from one time to the next if the book would work for me. Why I hadn't thought to ask the book this in the first place was beyond me, but that was beside the point now. The only bad part was that I had to remember the words. I wasn't sure if I could do it, and I knew if I got it wrong then it could end in disaster.

With no time to hide the book again, I reluctantly left it by the door and ran outside. Besides, I felt confident that they wouldn't be able to slip past me and inside to take the book. I looked around for my enemies, but they weren't there. Where had they gone this time? I looked back at the door and saw Giovanni walking into the manor. I'd left the book on the table by the door and now he was going to get his dirty hands on it. How could I be so stupid? I'd practically allowed it to fall right in to his trap.

I took off in a sprint. My side hurt from running so fast, but I couldn't stop now. I recited a spell in my mind to allow me move faster, and the next thing I knew, I was standing on the veranda. I stormed into the manor. I had no idea where the coven members were.

Giovanni was standing in the foyer when I entered, and sure enough, he had the book clutched in his arms.

He cackled when he looked at me. "You are too late. I have the book now. There is nothing you can do about it."

Panic surged through my body, but I couldn't let him win. I wasn't going to give up that easily. "You can't do anything with the book. You won't even be able to get it out of the house."

Giovanni rushed toward me and I wondered if he was going to attack me. Instead he pushed me to the side and forged toward the door. I knew he wanted to get the book to Kelley. I lifted my arms and pointed it at him. I tried my best to remember the words from the spell. How did that second sentence go? There was no time to debate it. I had to go with what I thought it was.

He was already on the front porch when I stormed out the front door. I continued to recite the words as I remembered them from the book and hoped that I got it right. Now more than ever I needed this to work. Where was everyone else? I didn't have a chance to even look around for them.

The first time I repeated the spell, he slowed down. His movements were in slow motion, so either I had it right or I was close. I had to recite the words again. This time he fell to his knees and the book landed next to him on the ground.

I rushed over and kicked it away from him so that I would have more time to grab it. He reached for me, but I'd moved just in time. I reached down and grabbed the book and clutched it tightly to my chest.

Giovanni stumbled to his feet. A vein near his left eye bulged as his face grew red. I started reciting the spell again and Kelley, Kevin, and the other woman appeared. That was when I spotted the coven members. They stood in a circle holding hands with a wispy white cloud floating above their heads like a vortex. The newly formed coven struggled to lift their arms and cast a spell my way, but they were powerless against the other coven.

Kelley and her gang of witches started walking toward the trees. They didn't look back, but instead they just marched across the yard, then disappeared behind one of the trees. Had they disappeared for good this time? I hoped so. I looked down at the book. Thank goodness it was safe. This scene had been uncannily like the last spell when the 1785 coven members and I had thought we'd gotten rid of Giovanni and Kelley. Was it finally over this time?

I hurried across the lawn toward the manor with the book in my arms. I had to get it back inside before something else happened. I glanced over my shoulder repeatedly to see if Kelley and the others had returned, but so far they weren't back.

After making it inside, I immediately took the book upstairs and locked it away in the trunk at the foot of my bed. I moved over to the window and looked out across the yard for Giovanni, but he wasn't there. Releasing a deep breath of relief, I placed the key for the trunk on a chain and slipped it around my neck. The key would be secure tucked under my shirt. I locked the door to my bedroom and headed back downstairs. Finally the book was secure in my room. No one would be able to get near it now.

The sound of the front door opening caught my attention. I held my breath waiting for movement. When I reached a place on the stairs where I could see downstairs, I spotted Nicolas in the foyer. The coven members stood around him with giddy smiles on their faces.

A smile immediately spread across my face. "Am I happy to see you," I said as I rushed down to hug him.

"We thought you were going to hug us," Rebecca said.

I released my hold on Nicolas and reached over for a group hug with the ladies. "I can't thank you all enough for what you've done."

"You're welcome, dear. At least now we know why we were here. You needed our help to fight the coven. Who else would be better to fight their symbol magic than a coven who used the same symbol magic?"

"What happened?" Nicolas asked, looking me up and down, then looking at the coven members. "You look like you've been in a fight."

I smoothed my hair down and nodded. "You could say that."

I explained about Kelley and her newly formed coven returning for the book. The coven members beamed as I recounted their heroic efforts. I wasn't so overjoyed though because I had no way of knowing if Kelley and her coven were truly gone for good. Only time could tell.

"What I want to know is how did Giovanni add the spells?" Nicolas asked.

"He'd unlocked the magic and created a spell that would allow him to add spells to the book. Kelley had been a part of an evil coven and had returned to seek revenge for having her leader status stripped away. She couldn't stand not having the power. She'd used Giovanni to get the book for her. She never intended on allowing him to be the leader. It figures the time when I'm put in charge is when all hell breaks out within the Underworld."

"I'm so sorry that I wasn't here for you." Nicolas caressed my cheek.

I shook my head. "You can't always be here, and apparently there is always something crazy going on around here."

"We'll leave you two alone," Rebecca said as the coven members walked across the room and in the direction of the kitchen.

"No magic spells in the kitchen," I called after them.

They'd just disappeared around the corner when the doorbell rang. I honestly didn't want to answer the door. It was never good news. In spite of my reluctance, I forced myself over to the front door.

Nicolas stood beside me in his ready-to-fight stance. He nodded. "Okay, I'm ready. Open the door."

With my hand on the doorknob, I released a deep breath and opened the door. Misty Middleton was standing in front of me. Nicolas relaxed his stance.

She smiled widely. "Hi, Hallie. How are you? You look great today. I like that sweater. Is it new?"

No amount of flattery would save her now. "What can I do for you, Misty?" I asked drily.

She paused, then said, "Look, Hallie, I know I betrayed you, and I am sorry, but you can forgive me, right?"

I shook my head. "I'm not sure I can do that, Misty."

She scowled. "Don't you believe in second chances?"

"Of course I do, but your actions have to have consequences." She stared at me blankly as if that concept was totally foreign. I continued, "I think you should be suspended as leader for the time being."

"What! You can't do that." Shock tightened he delicate features of her face.

"If you don't have any other mishaps, then we can discuss you being the leader again," I said.

Misty glared at me. Without a word, she spun around and stomped down the steps and to her car. She glared at me one last time as she hopped in her car and then took off down the driveway. Gravel spun out from behind the wheels. Misty was no longer leader of the coven. This left me with a dilemma. Who would be the leader? It would be a temporary position until Misty proved that she wasn't going to screw me over anymore.

The thought had barely left my head when Nicolas stepped closer to me.

"Misty was in a bit of a hurry." He gestured with a tilt.

I shook my head. "I guess getting the news that you're no longer the leader will do that to you."

He nodded. "It's the only thing you could do after what happened."

"Yeah, except now I need someone to replace her for the time being. I think she'll end up as the leader again, but in the meantime…" I looked at him.

He met my gaze. "What are you thinking?"

"I'm thinking what if you stayed in Enchantment Pointe as the leader of the coven for a while." I gave him a long, searching look.

"I think people will know that you gave me special treatment in giving me that position," he said.

"I know, but honestly, you are the most qualified person for the job."

Okay, so as far as I knew, there were no specific qualifications to be a coven leader. And to be honest, I had no idea Nicolas' true experience or skill level that would make him qualified for the position, but I trusted that he would be a great leader. Call it a hunch.

He stared at me, but didn't answer.

"It would be a favor to me, really." I smiled.

Nicolas rubbed my arms, sending a chill down my body. A tingly sensation zipped through my body when he leaned in closer and placed his warm lips against mine. Needless to say I melted into his kiss, allowing the stress to flow out of my body. It was hard not to succumb to his charm. The room began to spin as his tongue moved across mine. I pressed my body closer to his. Nicolas released me from his arms and grabbed my hand, leading me into the parlor.

"What's going on?" I asked. "Did something happen that you forgot to tell me about? It's more bad news, right? Of course it is. What else could it be?"

"Would you please calm down," he said with a smile in his voice.

I released a deep breath. "Okay. I'm calm. Now tell me what's going on."

He gestured toward the sofa. "Would you like to sit down?"

"Is the news that bad? Now I need to sit down?" I asked.

He quirked an eyebrow.

"I'm doing it again. But can you blame me?" I released another cleansing breath. "Okay. I'm ready." I eased down on the sofa, not taking my eyes off Nicolas. "So let me have it."

He grabbed my hands in his and looked me in the eyes. "I'd love to stay in Enchantment Pointe for a while, if the offer is still on."

A huge smile spread across my face. "Are you kidding? Of course the offer still stands. I just asked you, didn't I? I need you. I can't think of anyone more qualified."

"Well, I think you're just being biased, but I appreciate the compliment." Nicolas kissed me with a long soft kiss.

Annabelle burst through the door—without knocking or hesitating to come inside like a skittish cat. "I couldn't wait to tell you the news."

Okay, I could tell by the smile on her face that it was good news. Why couldn't Nicolas have given me that same look? He was always so serious.

"What's going on?" I jumped up and met her across the room.

Annabelle's eyes were wide and she was talking so fast that I couldn't understand her. I grabbed her hands. "Okay, tell me what's going on. The suspense is getting to me," I said.

"Remember the other day when we were at your mother's shop?" she asked.

I nodded. "Yes, I remember."

"Well, remember how I did the spell stuff with her," she said.

"Yeah." I nodded again.

"I was talking to your mom and she asked if I wanted to help her at the shop. I can't believe that I can do magic too."

I smiled. I never thought she'd be this excited over the paranormal. She'd always wanted to run in the opposite direction. But why she'd never known she had this special talent before now I didn't know. That was something I would have to find out.

I hugged her. "That's fantastic, Annabelle."

"Congratulations," Nicolas said. He pushed to his feet and closed the distance between them, shaking Annabelle's hand.

"Where's Jon?" I asked. He'd been almost invisible since I'd questioned him about his association with Kevin.

"Oh, he's in the car. He thinks you're mad at him."

"What? Why would I be mad at him? Tell him to come inside," I said.

Just as I'd erased the jumbled thoughts from my mind and given in to the happiness of the moment, we were interrupted by a loud rap on the door. Nicolas, Annabelle, and I froze, turning to gawk at the door. Who could it be? Had Kelley returned? Not another bed-and-breakfast guest, right?

I prayed it wasn't someone looking to take the Book of Mystics away. I'd hoped that I'd put that all behind me now. The knock had been loud as if someone really wanted in. That was the only sign I needed in order to know that this was going to be bad news. I jumped up and hurried to the front door.

Nicolas looked out, then looked back at me. "It's a woman."

"Oh no. Do you recognize her? Is it the woman we saw at the festival? Because she's a part of Kelley's coven."

Annabelle stood behind me, using me as a shield.

Nicolas shook his head. "No, I've never seen her before."

I'd let my guard down too soon. It had been wrong for me to think that this was over that easily. I couldn't get that lucky. I stepped over to the door and looked out. Nicolas was right. It wasn't the woman from the festival or anyone else who I recognized. That was odd. I eased the door open and looked at the woman.

"May I help you?" I asked.

She nodded with a little smile. She was a petite woman with long wavy hair and high cheekbones and gorgeous big brown eyes.

"I saw your bed-and-breakfast sign. You have a charming place here," she said.

This was not happening. There was no use in fighting it. I might as well invite her in.

"Please won't you come in?" I stepped out of the way so that she could enter.

Nicolas and I watched as she stepped across the threshold and placed her bag on the floor.

"This place is even lovelier on the inside," she said.

"Will you need to stay long?" I asked, hoping that she would say no.

I looked at her suspiciously. Nicolas was even giving her that same odd look. Annabelle leaned closer, waiting for her answer.

"Oh, I'm not here as a guest. I've been called here to investigate your recent magic," she said.

She didn't even look me in the eyes when she said this, as if this was an everyday occurrence. Had the leader ever been investigated before?

I was sure I had a confused look on my face. "What are you talking about?"

"You brought an entire coven back from the dead. They called us. They said they're not ever going back to the other dimension. We have a huge problem on our hands because of that. You really should watch your magic," she said sweetly.

I couldn't believe the coven members had called to rat on me.

"And who are you?" I asked.

"My name is Charlie Scott. I work as an Underworld investigator, but I like to call myself a full-time witch. The Underworld Board called me as soon as they heard from the coven members. You are under investigation."

I looked at Nicolas. He looked just as shocked as me.

"There's an Underworld Board? I knew there were small committees for each coven and such, but an actual board? Can the leader of the Underworld be under investigation?" I asked, looking from her to Nicolas for an answer.

"I'm afraid so," she answered. "Now if you'll please show me to my room." She picked up her bag and moved over to the staircase.

Well, I hadn't seen that coming, but honestly, I should have. I exchanged a look with Nicolas again. He shrugged.

"Can she do this?" Annabelle whispered.

I didn't answer because Charlie was staring right at me. After motioning for her to follow me, we made our way up the long and winding stairs.

Once I reached the second floor, I walked down the long hallway with the woman following me. At the second door down the hallway, I stopped in front of the door and unlocked it.

"Here you are." I motioned as I opened the door. "I think you'll find everything you need. There are towels in the bathroom."

She smiled. "Thank you. By the way, Hallie. I'm not here to give you a hard time. I'm sure this will all be cleared up in just a few days."

I nodded. "I'll talk to you soon."

Charlie started to close the door and I took that as my sign. I backed away from the door and made my way back down the hallway.

How would I get out of this mess?

ABOUT THE AUTHOR

Rose Pressey is a USA TODAY bestselling author. She enjoys writing quirky and fun novels with a paranormal twist. The paranormal has always captured her interest. The thought of finding answers to the unexplained fascinates her.

When she's not writing about werewolves, vampires and every other supernatural creature, she loves eating cupcakes with sprinkles, reading, spending time with family, and listening to oldies from the fifties.

Rose suffers from Psoriatic Arthritis and has knee replacements. She might just set the world record for joint replacements. She's soon having her hips replaced, elbows, and at least one shoulder.

Rose lives in the beautiful commonwealth of Kentucky with her husband, son, and three sassy Chihuahuas.

Visit her online at:
http://www.rosepressey.com
http://www.facebook.com/rosepressey
http://www.twitter.com/rosepressey

Rose loves to hear from readers. You can email her at: rose@rosepressey.com

If you're interested in receiving information when a new Rose Pressey book is released, you can sign up for her newsletter at http://oi.vresp.com/?fid=cf78558c2a. Join her on Facebook for lots of fun and prizes.

Made in the USA
Lexington, KY
06 October 2013